The Young and Violent

The Young and Violent

Vin Packer

PROLOGUE BOOKS

F + W Media, Inc.

Published in electronic format by
PROLOGUE BOOKS
an imprint of F+W Media, Inc.
10151 Carver Road
Blue Ash, Ohio 45242
www.prologuebooks.com

eISBN 10: 1-4405-3930-8
eISBN 13: 978-1-4405-3930-5
POD ISBN 10: 1-4405-5813-2
POD ISBN 13: 978-1-4405-5813-9

This work has been previously published in print format as a Gold Medal Book by
Fawcett Publications, New York, NY.

THE YOUNG
AND
VIOLENT

I

I got the rehabilitation blues
A bunch of screws
Down at the po-lice station
Put me on probation
Rehabilitation
Rehabilitation
Blues . . .
—A RED EYES DE JARRO ORIGINAL

THE KINGS OF THE EARTH live on Park Avenue in
New York City. They stand now on the wooden bridge at
99th Street, over the train tracks, looking out at the red
switch lights of the New York Central, and looking down
at their turf. Their turf belongs to them and they control
it. Their turf extends ten blocks along the left side of
Park, from 98th street on up into 109th, where it fringes
El Barrio, Spanish Harlem. Somewhere within this bound-
ary the Kings of the Earth live, and over it, they rule. In
all there are nineteen Kings; but here and now only two,
Tea Bag Perrez, and Red Eyes de Jarro, the War Counselors. They smoke, and watch, and wait for Rigoberto
Gonzalves—Gober—the King of Kings, their leader.

5

In the deep blue light of beginning evening a figure mounts the steps of the bridge, and thinking it is their leader approaching, they tense and turn to see.

"Naw, naw, it ain't Gobe," Tea Bag sighs impatiently. "S'only Detached Dan."

"Suppose he knows?" Red Eyes wonders.

"Either that or he's smellin'," Tea Bag answers.

The pair watch Dan Roan's approach. Dan is what social-welfare circles call a "detached" worker; a street-gang worker. He is employed by the Youth Board; a slender fellow in his early thirties, well over six feet, with sand-colored, close-cropped hair, a lean, sharp-boned face, and bright green almond-shaped eyes. Dan walks leisurely toward them, a burned-down cigarette clutched between his long, narrow fingers, a faint smile at the edges of his wide, strong mouth. He wears a gray flannel suit, a green wool sweater under the jacket, a white shirt and plain yellow tie.

"Hi, boys!"

"Dan."

"Hello, Dan."

"Nice night." Dan stands beside them now, looking down at the squalor that is upper Park Avenue. A lumbering vegetable truck squeezes its way in the close street beneath them, snorting and coughing smoky fumes and somewhere across from them in one of the tenement rooms a woman's husky voice croons, *"A room with a view—and you—"* The early May sky is not yet dark, but the red neons in the drugstore on the corner are shining, and the raggedy yellow tomcat from the grubby grocery next to it is locked inside, lying on a bunch of grapefruit in the display window, staring out moodily with his tail switching.

Dan says, "What's new?"

Tea Bag shrugs his shoulders. "They shot a bomb off at Yucca Flats, I hear. I hear tell they did that."

Tea is a short, medium-sized fifteen-year-old with mud-colored hair, a smooth, ruddy complexion, and a slumping posture. He is an alumnus of Coxsackie, a state correctional institution, and under the sleeves of his shiny black leather jacket his arms are punctured with needle marks. Before he went to Coxsack, he enjoyed a brief flirtation with marijuana and earned his nickname when his ma got in the habit of chiding him, "You're nothing but a bag of tea, sonny boy," but then he was only playing with the stuff. Now he has a romance with heroin, the white, white snow.

Dan stubs his cigarette out and tosses it over his shoulder, sticks his hands in his trousers pockets and rocks back and forth on his heels. "Yes, I read about Yucca Flats in the paper," he says quietly.

"Big explosion," Tea remarks.

"It's the time of the year for them," Red Eyes de Jarro says. "It's in the air."

Red Eyes wears a black jacket, too, with the same gold crown stamped on its back, and his name King de Jarro stenciled in white on the front above his heart. He is taller than Tea, but not truly tall, and he is thinner. His brown hair is darker, his large round eyes are darker. Red is far-sighted, so much so that the strain from the years he went without glasses gave his eyes the bleary, bloodshot appearance which inspired his name. Now he has glasses in an imitation leather case shoved in a drawer somewhere at home. In September he will be sixteen, old enough to quit school.

"That's the truth, Eyes," Tea Bag agrees. "It's in the air."

Dan addresses them seriously, "What's up, boys?"

"Gober's dinner when he finds out what happened," Tea tells him.

"Gober has a proprietary attitude toward his possessions," Red Eyes asserts.

"Meaning?"

"Meaning Babe Limon."

"Suppose you let me in on it, boys. You don't want another rumble. Is it something between the Kings and the Jungles again?"

Red Eyes unzips his jacket; and zips it up again, toying with the zipper as he talks. "Babe Limon is Gober's girl. You know that, Dan. It's a fact anyone knows. She's his property!"

"I never see them together much any more."

"Okay! So maybe he has a thing on some other broad, or something. I'm not saying he does or he doesn't, Dan, but Babe Limon is Gober's property, and the Jungles know that. They know that as well as they know their turf from our turf!"

"All right, Red. All right. Now, what's the deal? Did a Jungle try to cut in on Babe?"

"Not yet! And not just *a* Jungle. *The* Jungle did it, Dan—the leader, no less. Flat Head Pontiac!" Red Eyes scratches a match on the bridge's side, touches it to his cigarette, and sucks in smoke. He says, "Flat Head Pontiac's spread the word he's out to make Babe at the Friday-night dance."

"'At's right," Tea says. "Word's spread all over like grassfire."

"But he can't do it, boys, if Babe isn't willing."

Red Eyes sighs. "You don't get the point, Dan. Even if Babe isn't willing we lose face if we let Flat Head even try. Don't you see that? That's some gall Flat Head has, even to say a thing like that."

"Yeah," Tea Bag reflects. "Another thing. There's no tellin' 'bout that bitch, Babe. Like, she'd *enjoy* a rumble over her. She teases, you know? She might just come on strong with Flat Head to see the fireworks."

The threesome stand meditating momentarily, each thinking over the problem. In Dan's book a rumble is defined as an all-out mass gang fight, juvenile delinquency in the raw. But to Tea Bag and Red Eyes, to the Kings of the Earth and the Jungle Boys, to those and those like them, a rumble is Russian Roulette played with iron pipes and ball bats. It is violence "on the rocks," with the rocks stuffed inside socks, swung through the air at random and with malice. Or it is violence, neat, clean and quick as the flashing sharp blade of a switch knife or a straight razor. A rumble is a rumble. Red Eyes and Tea have fought and bled in rumbles, and seen boys drop beside them and get wasted by a bullet in their brains or a dagger in their guts.

"Look, boys," Dan says finally, "you're the war counselors of the Kings. Why don't you declare a talk with the Jungles; and if they have a grievance, arrange a fair fight?"

Tea gives a high, wild giggle to punctuate the impossibility of this suggestion. "What we supposed to say, Detached Dan? We supposed to say, 'Look here, Flat Head, you can fight for something that belongs to Gober if you wants to, but you got to fight fair, man.' That what we supposed to declare a talk about? How to cop another guy's broad by the rule book?"

Red Eyes slaps Dan's back good-naturedly. "The trouble with you, Dan," he says tolerantly, "is that you're too goddam detached. No, sir, if Flat Head does like he says and makes a play for Babe, there's just got to be a rumble."

A whistle hoots and a train roars toward them, down under them on the sooty tracks. Above the noise it makes, Dan tells Red Eyes to remember that he's on probation; and Red Eyes, singing loudly so the engines don't drown him out, chants: *"Re-habil-i-ta-tion, re-ha-bil-i-ta-tion, rehabilitation—bull-lew-oohs!"* Tea laughs with his shoulders shaking, and spits down at the train; and Dan Roan watches the pair through tired, thoughtful eyes.

Then the train has passed on into the distance; and it is quiet and getting darker.

"Wonder what's keeping Gobe?" says Tea. "Gang's all up in the cellar waitin'."

"Maybe he's gone on up there," says Red Eyes.

"Naw, I tole him to come here. Tole him we wanted to talk to him before the meetin'. Figured be better he get it from us first."

"Then he's probably delayed," Red Eyes states flatly.

"Yeah, like you know he is, man—and by *who* he is too, I'm hip!"

"I don't know that for sure, Tea. You don't either."

"It ain't my business."

"Darn right."

"A broad is only a broad, so who cares?"

"You don't even know that, Bag."

"Am I arguing?"

They talk, ignoring Dan Roan. They talk freely before him, knowing he will not stool; unsure about what he hopes to gain by hanging in their turf with his mild, impartial ways, his calm, persistent reasoning, and his undemanding and perpetual concern for them. There was a time when they were suspicious of this man, in the very beginning when he first showed up night after night in their haunts—the candy stores, restaurants and pool halls where the Kings concentrate. D.&D., the mute who is the Kings' scout, followed Roan and observed him two weeks straight, and came back and wrote what he knew. "Seem o.k. . . . Clame to be sochal workor . . . Talk with kids . . . Dont buddy with cops . . . Seem o.k."

"Still and all," Gober had decided, "keep him at arm's length. He might be an undercover narcotics agent."

"Or a plain-clothes Friday," Tea had suggested.

"Or a pigeon," another King had speculated.

"Or a fag."

Dan Roan's acceptance by the Kings of the Earth was slow, and never quite complete. Tea Bag was still prone to put him down now and then, though Tea knew Dan was aware of his romance with the white snow, and had never turned him in or slipped his name to the feds. Just on principal, Tea was hot and cold with Dan, because he'd learned at Coxsack that a hophead had to be careful. About these social guys, Tea had a slogan: "Let them help you if they can; but don't you help them if you can."

The King of Kings—Gober—said Dan Roan was all right so long as he knew his place, and he stayed lukewarm with him all the time. Most of the Kings followed suit. Red Eyes dug Dan more than the others; in fact, Dan was the only person in the world besides Red Eyes' girl who knew that Red Eyes' ambition was to be a lyricist.

Dan listens as they talk; waiting until they have chewed down the subject of Gober's delay, and paused, and again scanned the narrow streets beneath them for a sign of Gober, anxiously now, and silently.

To Red Eyes, Dan says, "Still want to go on Thursday night?"

"I'll think about it," Red Eyes answers noncommittally.

"Well, let me know. If you don't, I'll take my wife."

Red Eyes snorts. "She sleeps with you; I don't. Maybe you ought to." He is embarrassed before Tea to discuss the matter.

"What happens on Thursdee night?" Tea Bag grins. "Second honeymoon trip to Gibralter, somethin'?"

"Sure, sure," Eyes tells him. "How'd you know?"

"No kiddin', what gives Thursdee?"

"Someone at the Youth Board came up with tickets for a show," Dan says. "I told Red Eyes he could come along with me if he liked."

Red Eyes blushes and mumbles, "My mind isn't made up."

"Oh yeah? Big Bro'way show? I never seen one."

"Well, maybe next time—" but Dan does not finish.

Tea says, "Naw, naw, Christ, naw. S'for the birds. Who needs it, huh? Who needs it?"

"I might be busy Thursday anyway," Eyes says. "Things are in the air."

"Where de hell is Gobe, f'Chrissake!" Tea complains. "Delay, delay, only I bet it don't lay. Not the stuff he's chasin'."

Eyes tells Bag he's asking for it, to talk too much.

"Did I say anything?" Bag says innocently. "Did you hear *me* say somethin'?"

The sky grows dark; and from a television set off behind them, a commentator barks out news in a clipped jumble of words. Dan Roan pushes back his coat sleeve and holds his arm to the light to see his watch. He whistles and says, "Whew! It's late."

Red Eyes feels bad the way he talked to Roan. His voice is polite. "Do you have to meet your wife at the church, Dan?"

"Yes, in about an hour. But I have to stop somewhere else first. I'd better run along."

"I'll let you know, Dan," Eyes says.

"Do that, Red Eyes." Roan clamps his hand on Red Eyes' arm. "A rumble won't do you any good at all; you know that, don't you?"

"What can I do? If the Kings rumble, I gotta rumble, Dan. I can't punk out."

"You're not punking out. It isn't like punking out. You're on probation and you can't afford to rumble."

Tea says, "So he's on probation, f'Chrissake. What's that? You say you go school. 'At's what they want you to say. You say you home every night ten o'clock. 'At's what they want you to say. You tell 'em what they want to hear, 'at's all. F'Chrissake, an old Coxsack alum like me get caught, I gotta go to Warwick for post graduate work. Probation! F'Chrissake! What's that?"

Dan says, "Red Eyes knows what it is. He knows what it means."

"Still, I gotta rumble, Dan, if they decide. I'm a King. Hell, I'm a War Counselor."

"You think it over," Dan tells him, "and tell Gober I'd like to talk with him during the week. Some time before Friday. Will you tell him?"

"Sure, Dan."

Tea Bag says, "Probation, f'Chrissake!"

In his pocket Red Eyes has a dog-eared letter he has

received from the Arco Music Publishers of America.
Since Dan arrived he has wanted to show it to him to get
his opinion, but around Tea he is unwilling to mention it.
Now as Dan starts away he fingers it without taking it
out of his jacket, wondering if he should run ahead and
show Dan. But Dan walks fast, and Tea is curious like an
undertaker reading the obits. Tomorrow maybe. The next
day.

As Dan starts down the bridge's wooden steps, Tea Bag
calls, "You see Gobe up round Ninety-seventh in a certain place, you tell him hot-foot it over here, huh, Dan?
You going that way? Where you going?"

"I'm not going in that direction, Perrez, sorry." Dan
waves "I'm going to see a friend."

Tea Bag shouts, "Oh yeah? I ought to go along with
you. I never seen one of them!"

Then the Kings of the Earth, Tea and Eyes, stand in
the darkness closing around them, up above their turf, and
await the King of Kings.

II

*Rigoberto Gonzalves—in the
words of the gang he led, "Gober,"
"the boss," "the King of Kings"
but in plain words, a hood, a
hoodlum, a punk!*
—FROM "WHY PAMPER PUNKS?" A COLUMN
IN THE NEW YORK JOURNAL-AMERICAN.

INSIDE the luncheonette at the corner of 97th and Madison Avenue, Gober straddles a stool at the fountain, sips slowly his fourth cup of coffee, and watches her. Outside on the curb, Junior Brown sits holding Gober's leather jacket across his lap, munching on a cold fried frog's leg he has pulled from a greasy brown paper sack.

It is ten minutes before nine.

She waits on a party in a booth, then walks back behind the fountain to wash dishes stacked in the aluminum sink. Gober says to her, "You could talk to a guy, at least."

Gober is seventeen, husky and tall, with tangled black hair and deep brown eyes. He has a dark, handsome face, and an uncertain smile which tips his thin lips.

Her name is Anita and she is beautiful. To Gober she is like a girl the *marceros* would serenade, back in Rio Piedras, during the feast of Marza, when they would roam the streets singing on their *rondas*. Gober could still remember that about home, though he had left there four years ago. He could still remember the sound of the guitars, strummed by the soft-voiced young men who sang, *"Bello, pulido alelí, no me trates de olvidar . . ."* pleading, "Beautiful, dainty gilliflower, do not try to forget me . . ."

Whenever Gober is near her, he thinks of her always in Spanish, and he thinks that he would like to talk to her in that language, not in English; and sometimes, like now, when she does not answer him, he does.

"No me mires con enojo," he tells her.

13

She turns and looks at him. Her raven-colored long hair is knotted with ribbon in a horsetail, and her white skin is smooth and burnished. She seems to shine; her dark eyes are coal-shaded and lustrous, her lips full and wide, and red without lipstick; her profile madonnalike in its serene perfection. Medium in height, she has a young, ripe body, slender and rounded, which fills her crisp white uniform fully, and legs that are long, shapely and slender.

"You know I don't understand you," she says.

"I say, don't look at me angry."

"He'll come here soon, that's all."

"What have I done he should act that way to me?"

"Pop doesn't like gang boys. It's worse since that boy in the Bronx got killed last week by a gang boy."

"*I* didn't kill him."

"But a gang boy did. It's no good, Gober. He'll have a fit if he finds you here."

"Then, later meet me. I—"

"No," she says firmly. "There's no way. It's no good, Gober!"

He says, "I'm not wearing my jacket—" but she walks away from him to the booth in the back, and stands writing out the check for the party there.

The jukebox whines a torch song and Gober sits despondently thinking that this whole thing happened to him because he had a lousy hole in his molar. Two weeks ago he never saw her; then when he was passing this luncheonette ten days past, he stopped to buy penny gum to stuff a cavity, and the hamburger grill was smoking, and there was nobody in the place besides her and him. So he showed her how to scrape it, and told her about making sure there weren't any meat scraps left to burn once she'd cooked something on it; and they got to talking. Now he was hooked worse than Tea was on snow, and she was just as hard to get.

"You keep out of this place, King Gonzalves," her old man had said, eying Gober's jacket, the first time he had seen Gober in the luncheonette. And the third time Gober had gone there he said, "I don't want your kind hanging around here!"

"What's my kind?" Gober had asked him.

"Young punks with Sam Browne belts holding their britches up, and knives and rock weighing them down.

King! Not here! Not around here you don't play king!"
Mr. Manzi had barked.

Beside Gober's arm on the counter there is a pencil, and
sipping his coffee, he eyes it, picks it up, and turns it in
his thick, square fingers. From the silver dispenser he
pulls a napkin and begins to draw. Behind him he hears
the party in the booth laughing and the music asking where
the baby's dimple will be, and the whir of the electric
fan. He draws a picture of a small curly-headed boy
staring in the window of a café at a large *rulino*, a Spanish
meat pie. The boy's eyes are round and wide and wistful.
Gober studies his picture momentarily, a faint smile playing on his mouth, and then underneath he scribbles the
caption: *No sabe como te quiero*—You don't know how
much I love you. Then he looks up for Anita, and sees
her standing down at the far end of the fountain.

"Nita. I have something funny to show you."

She shakes her head, not looking at him.

He whispers, *"Psss*—please!" and he is smiling, but she
says only, "Go, Gober. Please go before Pop comes!" and
does not move from her place there.

For a while he looks steadily at her, hoping she will
turn her head toward him, come down to him, or say
something more, but she is adamant. He drinks the rest
of his coffee without taking his eyes from her, wipes
his mouth on another napkin and sighs. He sees the clock;
a few minutes before nine, and remembers his appointment at the bridge—with Eyes and Tea. Still for some
seconds he stays, persisting in his hopes, which are in vain
—and then, resigned, he sighs a second time, swings off the
high stool, and stands regarding his drawing. Again he
calls her, "Nita, I left something for you," and shoving
the napkin down the counter, he ambles toward the door
and out into the street.

Pausing before the windows of the luncheonette, Gober
reaches into the pocket of his clean white shirt for a
cigarette, finds it, sticks it between his lips, and flips
a match into flame with his thumbnail. A few feet from
him, squatting on the curb, Junior Brown exclaims, "Hey
—'bout time, Gobe. You been forever!"

Junior Brown is an undersized fourteen-year-old, with
skin the color of milk chocolate, eyes like round brown
marbles; teeth that are straight and buck and white as
alabaster, and black burred hair. He looks up at Gon-

zalves with reverence and awe, and holds Gonzalves' jacket as though it were the seamless coat of Christ, and grinning uncontrollably, he says, "You git to talk to her, man?"

Gober glances sideways and sees her staring out at him, and for a moment they look straight at each other that way, oblivious to everything else, searching one another's eyes with painful excitement, until after what seems to them to be a long time, Anita Manzi turns her back on Gonzalves. Drawing in on his cigarette, Gober exhales a cloud of smoke and stands stonily.

"You gonna be late, Gobe," Junior Brown tries again.

"Give me my jacket, Nothin' Brown!" Gober snaps authoritatively, "and never mind the small talk!"

Then Gober straightens his shoulders, assumes a new and more characteristic posture, and saunters toward the younger boy, holding his long arms out for Brown to slip on the black jacket. "C'mon, Nothin'," Gober says in his old, sure voice, "I got business to attend to t'night. Let's make tracks!"

The pair stride down Madison Avenue, Brown a foot behind Gonzalves, his big eyes fixed on his idol's back. Brown is not a King, for the Kings of the Earth have no colored "citizens," but, undaunted, he is an accessory whose skinny stick legs, like taut pistons, drive him on, following relentlessly in Gober's tracks. Two years ago, when his mother and he had moved from 127th Street down into El Barrio, and he'd gone his first day to P.S. 109, he'd achieved a certain small notoriety among his classmates.

"What did you say your name was?" the teacher had asked him a second time at roll.

"Junior Brown, ma'am."

"Your first name?"

"Junior."

"What's the Junior stand for?" she had persisted.

"It stands for nothin'," he'd answered.

"Well," she said impatiently, "what's your father's first name?"

"Ma'am, I don't have one of those. My mother named me." So they had come to call him simply "Nothin'."

"You headin' off for the cellar, Gobe?" Brown questions.

"Meeting Eyes and Bag first. What're you eating, Nothin'? What're you sucking on there?"

Junior Brown held out the paper sack. "Want one, Gobe?"

"What is it?"

"Frogs' legs."

"Ugh! Christ, no! Where'd you steal them from?"

"No, sir, I didn't swipe 'em. My mother give 'em me. She get 'em from where she work."

"Yeah?"

"Yeah, she a domestic."

"Yeah?"

"Yeah, she get all sorts things. T-bone steak once."

"Yeah?"

"Sure! She get all sorts things!"

In his excitement at capturing Gober's interest, Junior Brown babbles on about the shad roe he had once, and the venison, the lobster tail, and the ar'choke; but Gonzalves is not hearing any of it. His brow is knit in a frown, his concentration on something else, impervious, as they cross Madison and head down 98th in the direction of Park. Above them in the windows of the dilapidated apartment buildings, people lean on pillows on the ledges staring out at one another, and down at the squalor of the sidewalks and pavement beneath them. Shoeless kids play with fire at a rubbish heap on the corner, and a half a dozen men squat around a crap game midway in the block. A woman sits lazily on a front stoop, her breast bared and offered to her baby, cradled in her arms; while a fat, yawning friend sits in a camp chair chatting with her. Through the jagged glass of a broken window in a street-floor flat, an old man peers out; behind him a television set shows dancing bears on its screen as a flute plays *Rio Rita,* and a small girl in the room blows bubble gum into a pink balloon and skips rope. A street light that has been stoned out makes the end of the block dark, and in this darkness there are the shadows of others lingering idly, yakking and laughing and looking at what there is to see.

". . . and Missus Morganhotter tell my mother, 'Take 'em Bessie. We going Connetick this weekend and won't eat 'em anyways,'" Junior Brown is reciting to Gonzalves as they move along, "and them pok chop was three inch thick and wide as all outdoors and——"

But Gober interrupts suddenly, barking, "Nothin'!"

"Huh?"

"I want to tell you something!"

"What, Gobe?"

"I'll break your head in half, Nothin' Brown, if you say to *anyone* where I was tonight! You got that?"

"Man, you don't have to spell that out for me, and that's a fact!"

"I just wanted to make it clear."

"I know that much."

"Okay."

They cut around the corner of 98th and head up Park toward the wooden bridge that crosses the avenue, upon which Eyes and Bag wait. Nothin' Brown empties the chewed bones from the paper sack into the street and blows the bag up, punching it with his fist so it explodes. He giggles, "Got ya, ya stool!" and tosses the torn sack over his shoulder. Then he says, "Gobe?"

"What?"

"Can I go up far as the cellar with you? I ain't gonna snoop around. Just wanna walk up with you."

"I told you, Nothin', I got to have a confab with Eyes and Bag on the bridge first."

"I could wait till you was through, and then walk up with you to the meetin', Gobe. Can I?"

"Uh-uh."

"Sure wish you'd let me, Gobe."

"Uh-uh. This is King business!"

"You think there gonna be a rumble comin' up, Gobe?"

"You playing Twenty Question, Nothin'?"

"No, sir."

"Then don't!"

At the foot of the steps leading up to the bridge, Gober stops and looks down at Brown. "This is as far as you go," he says.

"I see you tomorrow?"

"If I don't see you first."

Nothin' Brown grins helplessly, nodding his head and backing off from Gonzalves with his puny hands tucked in the pockets of his worn brown corduroy pants. "Then I be seeing you, Gobe," he says. "S'long, Gobe."

Gober gives an easy salute and starts up the steps when suddenly Brown snaps his fingers, slaps his head, calls, "Gobe!"

"Yeah?"

"Forgot to tell you somethin'."

"Well?"

"Well, while you was in there, you know, while you was in the—"

"Yeah, yeah," Gober says impatiently, "what happened?"

"That Babe—she and this other broad come by, see, and they looks in at you, you know?"

Gober comes down from the step and walks over to Brown.

"What do you mean, they looked in at me."

"They just did. They looks in, and this broad, she says to Babe, 'See, what I tell you?' and Babe, she say, 'Yeah, yeah'—like that, you know?"

"Like what?" Gober demands.

"Like she was learnin' somethin', Gobe. She say real slow, 'Yeah, yeah.' You know?"

"And then?" Gober's voice rises.

"And then nothin'. They just go on then."

"That's all?"

"Sure. I sittin' there and I see 'em, and this broad say to Babe, 'See, what I tell you?' and Babe look and say, 'Yeah, yeah.' That's all. I thought you want to know."

"Thanks!" Gonzalves says.

"Well, I be seeing you t'morrow, Gobe. I be seeing you round."

Gonzalves does not answer. Slowly he climbs the wooden steps to the top, where the War Counselors await him.

Leaning against the pinball machine in the candy store on 100th and Madison, Babe Limon smokes a cigarette, and feigns interest in the June issue of *True Confessions*, which she has grabbed from the magazine rack behind her. As she flicks through the slick-paper pages, her friend Marie Lorenzi talks.

She says, "He own you or something? He contributing to your support, or something? He married to you or something?"

She files down her long red nails with angry motions. "Jesus, Babe, you saw him sitting there looking like he was swallowing blood over her! You going to take that?"

Babe Limon is a small sixteen-year-old with firm, full breasts, a lushly curved young body, soft, golden skin, brown hair piled on top of her head, and a pretty face which is overpainted with pancake, rouge, mascara, and lipstick. She wears a flared bolero jacket of a shiny pink color, a plaid wool skirt, and a bright silk striped blouse. Her ensemble is completed by a pair of worn black patent leather pumps, and a cheap gold charm bracelet is fastened around one ankle of her bare legs.

"One thing about Flat Head Pontiac," she says, still looking down at the magazine, "is that he *asked* me, you know what I mean? He comes up to me in the corridor at school, and he says, 'What'd you say if I said I was going to cut Gober out at the shindig Friday?' See? He gets my opinion. I says, 'You think you can? You think you can, Pontiac?' I just ask him if he thinks he can."

"You got to decide, Baby-O. I tell you, break with Gober! Everybody and his brother knows he cruising that Polack up in the ice cream parlor. He just comes to you to cool off!"

Marie stands arms akimbo as she talks, a tall, skinny, flat-chested girl in tight black slacks and a bright red sweater, a plastic raincoat drawn around her shoulders, a kerchief tied under her chin, and white socks and black toeless heels on her feet. She too wears a great deal of make-up, but her features are harder and more irregular than Babe's; and she looks more sure, somewhat mean, and slightly coarse in contrast.

"Last time I'm with Gober," Babe starts, as she lays the magazine across the pinball machine and folds her arms across her chest thoughtfully, "he tells me, 'Wash your face!' in just that kind of voice. Like it was an order. 'Wash your face!' We're down in the clubroom on the couch, all by ourselves, and he comes out with that. I say, 'What's eating you?' and he says, 'I'm not interested in making the cosmetic counter at Woolworth's.'"

"Gober said that?"

"Yeah. Three nights ago, after the dance. When I wore my blue."

"He doesn't appreciate you, Baby-O. He never did!"

"No, he *did*. He used to. I don't know what happened."

"It's that Polack, Baby-O."

"Yeah," Babe Limon agrees, "it's her, all right. But he don't get no place with her. That's what I don't understand. It's not like Gober. Geez, Marie, you don't know Gober! He's oversexed or something, know what I mean?"

"That's what I been trying to tell you, Baby-O. He just uses you. You'd think you were his wife, kid. You're crazy to torch for Gonzalves! Dime a dozen, Baby-O!"

Babe tosses her cigarette to the floor and squashes it out. "Flat Head has pimples," she says.

"So what! He's a big man! He's got a car, hasn't he?"

"Another thing Gober says to me last time we're together. You know how Gober is—always drawing these pictures of things?"

"Yeah, I know how Gober is—so?"

"So, he draws these two pictures of cats, see? One was a cat chasing in circles after his own tail. The other was a cat jumping up in the air trying to catch a rubber ball on a string that was too high for him to reach, see?"

Marie snorts, "What an imagination!"

"No, I mean, then he says to me, 'Baby, if you were a cat which one you rather be?' See? And I say the cat chasing his tail, cause it's more like a game, you know what I mean? Lots of cats play that way. One we got in our building is always chasing his tail. So I told him I'd rather be that one than the other one, because the other one couldn't get the ball he was after, do you see?"

"So what did Mr. Picasso say to that?"

"Well, he said, 'That's the difference between you and me, Baby. That's what makes horse races!' Then he gives me this whack across my rump, like he was being cute, only it was a hard whack, and he says, 'Why don't you clear out now, tootsie. Me and the boys got to huddle.' "

"You see!"

"It was two things in particular, Marie, if you follow me. It was all that stuff about the cats, like I'd chosen the wrong one or something. And then, it was the way he came on with this tootsie business, like I was just another girl and he was finished with me for the night, and I could go on home or drop dead or something."

"I follow you," Marie says. "Oh, I get the picture, all right." She points her nail file at Babe and tells her, "Chuck Gober! Play up to Flat Head, Baby-O, and let 'em rumble over you. That'll show Señor Gonzalves. Maybe he'll get a rock in his head!"

"You think the Kings would rumble over this?"

"Baby-O, they'd have to! It isn't like Gober announced to the world he threw you over. You're still Gober's girl on the books, Babe!"

"A rumble!" Babe Limon says thoughtfully.

"Sure, Baby-O. They'd have to!"

"A rumble," Babe repeats. "A rumble over me!"

III

*They are children and they need
our help. They are children and
they need our love. Are our children so
hard to help and love?*
—REV. ROBERT RICHARDS, ADDRESSING A
FORUM ON JUVENILE DELINQUENCY.

So I says who the Christ needs ta go ta a whore and
take de chance gettin' rolled when you can get a bim any
night de week in a line-up for one skin!"

". . . and just when D.&D.'s got dis hub cap off the
Caddy's wheel, a lousy Friday shows and says you're unner
arres'!"

". . . tole me all dey do out on Nort Brudders Island for
a hoppy is give 'im de cold turkey treatment, f'Chrissake!"

The smoke pall is heavy in this cellar on 102nd Street
where the Kings are congregated. There are a dozen Kings
here—sitting on broken chairs, orange crates, a moth-eaten
couch with its springs popping from its insides, and a long
board supported at each end by empty beer barrels. A
naked, dinky electric light hangs on a cord from the ceiling, over a tottering card table at one end of the wide-
brick-walled room. Comic magazines are scattered about,
along with dice, cards, empty beer and pop bottles, and
old blankets.

This is their clubhouse, and it is not much, but they are
lucky to have it. The cellar where the Kings meet is safe;
and so are the goods of the newsdealer above them, who
lets them use the cellar in return for their guarantee that
his store will be "protected." Still, though they have per-
mission to be there, they are wary of the suspicious nature
inherent in coppers, and so they post Owl Vasquez outside, as lookout.

It is Owl who stills the room now.

He sticks his head in the door and shouts, "Gobe's here!"

There is a scraping of chairs as the Kings pull their sun-

22

dry seats up nearer to the card table; and the raucous hub-bub diminishes to a murmuring undertone, silenced completely in seconds when Owl shouts again: "On your feet! The King of Kings!"

Into the room Gober stalks, followed by Red Eyes de Jarro and Tea Bag Perrez. Gober looks neither right nor left, and at no one, but marches to the card table, while Eyes and Bag take chairs at his side. The Kings stand until Gober snaps, "Places!" and then there is silence, while Gober comes around in front of the table and paces silently.

"All right!" he says finally, facing all of them, "We got a crisis on our hands. Maybe you know—maybe you don't. We'll get to it after regular business. Let's clean up the usual first. Okay. Braden here?"

Braden stands up.

"What's the latest from your end, Braden?"

Braden is in charge of reporting any arrests made of Kings, of any sentencing of Kings in court, and of any imminent release of a King from a correctional school or reformatory.

"They picked up D.&D. last night, Gober! Held him over for court tomorrow."

"Yeah? What was he doing?"

"He was borrowing a hub cap from a big yellow Caddy."

"Christ, doesn't he know by now there's no future in hub caps! So he gets ten stinking cents for one! How many's he expect to get in one night."

Braden shrugs. "He got thirty a couple nights ago."

"So three dollars! Big deal!"

"Yeah, Gobe, but it's chow for D.&D. S'gotta eat."

"Yeah, yeah," Gober admits tiredly. "They questioning him about the gang? Anyone with him?"

"Naw, he was solo, and I don't think they're going to question a dummy long, particularly D.&D. You know him, Gober—they write the question down for him on a piece of paper, and then pass the paper to him. They write something like: Who do you sell your loot to? Braden pauses, shaking with laughter, and then says, "And D.&D. writes back to them, What? Whatta character, huh!"

Impatiently Gober snaps, "Okay. Okay. What else?"

"Just Morales," Braden says. "They sent him out to North Brothers Island for the cure."

"That's a good place for Morales," Gober asserts. "He'll

get more horse out there than he could get around here, and he'll be out of our hair. I hate a guy who's hooked that way. Now, take me. I sniff a little horse now and then, maybe I smoke some tea. I've been known to take a cap of the snowy stuff too. But I don't let it hook me. Or take Bag, here." Gober turns toward Perrez and Perrez nods and smiles blandly. "Bag's an addict. We all know that. Bag's got a mistress and her name is snow. But Bag doesn't let her make him so goddam daffy he walks off a roof or into the river. Bag keeps her to himself, and that's the way it should be. But Morales! He didn't know how to get the stuff. Pretty soon he'd steal and get picked up—and then he'd tell anything he knew if the coppers would promise him a cap of the snow. Morales should *stay* on North Brothers!"

Braden says, "You're right, Gober!"

Other Kings comment: "That's a fact!" "I'll buy that." "I can hear that coming in fine." "You tell them, Gober!"

"Okay, okay!" Gober yells. "This is a meeting! You finished, Braden?"

Braden gives a lazy salute and sits down.

"Flash, you're next. What's on the social agenda this week?"

Flash pulls himself up from the couch and stands knife-thin and tall, and dressed the way Flash always dresses, in the new "sweet" style of gangland, which has replaced the old zoot suit. He is a symphony in dark brown and tan. Flash dresses six nights out of a week. To support his liking for high fashion, Flash sells numbers, and pimps.

"Well, Kings," Flash drawls, "if anyone's interested there'll be a midnight revue on Tuesday, around quarter to midnight, here. It'll cost you two skins, and—"

"Two skins, fer the love of—" someone protests.

"Who's gonna shell out two skins for a line-up broad, for Christ—"

"You silly! Two skins! Who you pimping for, the Queen of Sheba?"

Flash holds up his hands for silence; and Gober booms, "Shut up and hear him out. Nobody's forcing the piece on you!"

Flash waits until the Kings are reasonably quiet. Then he continues: "Two bucks is a fair price for the bim I got lined up. One, this bim is a real doll—packed! Two, she isn't local talent. She's out-a-town pussy, in visiting relatives. Three, this bim is virgin territory!" Flash polishes his nails on his coat sleeve in a triumphant gesture, blows on them, raises an eyebrow and adds, "So I say you're lucky to get off for for two skins—I'd charge an outsider five. Quarter to twelve—here—Tuesday, if you're buying it."

"Okay!" Gober says. "We heard the announcement. Anything else!"

"Just the usual dance on Friday," Flash says, "and I hope you Kings'll be sweet from head to toe, cause as you know the Jungles have been putting more emphasis on the matter of wardrobe lately, and by comparison we look like a bunch of goddam slobs!"

Flash takes his seat again, and Gober resumes his pacing; talking now as he does. "That should clean the important business off the agenda now, while we deal with the most important business of all—a new development. Red Eyes de Jarro will at this time give a brief summary for those who may not have heard what's in the wind."

Red Eyes stands importantly before them; his legs spread, his arms behind his back. "Kings," he begins solemnly, "the general story is that Flat Head Pontiac Moravia has passed along the information he's out to make Babe at the Friday night dance." Red Eyes takes a breath after exploding this bomb, surveys the room through solemn eyes, and continues. "Kings," he says, "we all know this is top insult; and coming from a Jungle chief, aimed deliberately at our leader, it's unexcusable!"

The light from the naked bulb glints on Red Eyes' face as he pauses for emphasis and waits until the uprise of indignant murmuring subsides. Behind him, Gober sits at the card table with a blank expression on his face, showing no reaction whatsoever to his words. It is further proof of his perpetual poise; another indication of his sterling predisposition for leadership.

"I took an analysis of this situation," Red Eyes goes on, "along with Tea Bag, my fellow War Counselor, and it is the conclusion we came to that there is no way out but to rumble. What Pontiac intends is a straight insult through and through. We lose face not to war over it. That's my analysis. I now open the floor to discussion."

Gober pounds on the card table for silence. "One comment at a time!" he shouts; as the Kings begin talking all at once.

Two Heads Pigaro begins, "I don't dig fighting for some goddam broad, with no intent to critic you, Gobe. I just—"

"Stand up!" Red Eyes shouts. "This is a meeting!"

"So all right!" Two Heads stands. "I'm no chicken, and nobody ever said I was the type to punk out. I go into a rumble with as much guts as the next guy, but I always contended no broad is worth getting your head cracked open for, or your guts spilled on 107th street! S'far as I figure a rumble is when a wise guy invades your turf, not your goddam piece, cause if your piece can be had what good is it? You might as well get in line behind the others for a bim as try to—"

For the first time during this meeting, Bag becomes enraged. He jumps up and shouts at Two Heads, "What you know? You never had nothin' but a bim. You don't know the score on nothin' but a bim. You don't know—"

"I don't know what?" Two Heads holds his ground and snarls, "What you know? Is that what I don't know? You sleep with a goddam needle, hop head! You screw a goddam hypodermic—"

Gober hits the table with his fist again, almost breaking its legs. "Ask for the floor when you got something to say, you hear? What kind of lousy parliamentary procedure is this crap!"

"I'm just trying to tell this creep he never had nothin' but a bim," Tea Bag says. "Anything he ever had, he had to share!"

"Shut up!" Gober commands. "Red's got his hand up! That's the way to get the floor."

Red Eyes de Jarro waits for complete silence. Then he says carefully, "Look, Kings, let's make this clear right now! It's not a broad we're fighting over, see? It's not Babe! It's the insult! It's the idea a Jungle thinks he can walk right up to a King's deb and cut the King out! I call that nerve, see? I call that raw nerve!"

"Still," Two Heads persists, "it involves a broad!"

"No, Two Heads, it involves our honor. You ought to see that!"

"Him!" Bag nags. "He's thick in the head, f'Chrissake! Him know anything about honor, f'Chrissake?"

"I told you about asking for the floor, Bag!" Gober warns.

Blitz Gianonni raises his hand and gets the floor. "If you ask my opinion," he says, "the consensus is that since that crappy model boy got bumped off up in the Bronx, the heat is on, and a rumble is asking for a pad in a cell. I say Gober oughta forbid Babe to go to the dance Friday, and that way avoid all trouble."

"That's punking out, Blitz, and you know it," Red Eyes states.

"It is not, cause nothing's gonna happen that way."

Red Eyes moans, "How'm I gonna make you guys see? How?"

"Who needs to see!" someone shouts. "I'll rumble right now!"

"Yeah, I'm in!"

"It's clear as crystal!"

"Man, this is Rumbleville, s'far as I see it!"

"Let's go, hey!"

"Errrrrrrrumble! Yeah, yeah!"

Gober stands and glares at the Kings of the Earth until they are quieted. "I wish," he says with a pained expression, "that you guys would conduct yourself as guys in a meeting are supposed to. Now, let's face facts! It is clear that the majority is for a rumble, and that the majority sees this is a rumble not over Babe, but over the insult offered up on a silver platter by Flat Head Pontiac. Is that clear?"

A chorus of loud voices shouts, "Right!"

"And it is clear that this is an insult directed not at me personally, but at each and every King. Otherwise Pontiac would not announce his intentions. Clear?"

"Right!"

"So what chance do we have? To chicken, or to rumble. Right?"

"Right!"

"And do we chicken?"

"Hell, no!"

Gober socks the fist of one hand into the palm of another. "So there you are," he says. "There you are. Anyone got more to say?"

"When we gonna plan it for, Gobe?"

"I'm not sure in my mind about that," Gober says. "That's got to be thought out. But my best theory at the moment is that we ought to fall in at the dance, just like any other time, and let Pontiac make his play for my Babe —who I am going to have a sweet little talk with in person ahead of time. Then—after he has made his pitch, and after we have concluded dancing, and after the Jungles leave the hall—*then!*"

Flash pulls himself up from the couch again. "What about our clothes, man? We going to rumble in our sweet clothes?"

"I figure," Gober paces as he talks, "that we leave our rumble clothes here. We go in our sweet clothes, and we conduct like nothing is gonna happen that night, and we even let drop phrases like, 'Wait until tomorrow night!' to give them the idea we plan a rumble on Saturday. We carry on at the dance normal, and a few of us even drop in at the poolhall after, and we don't act excited—but we beat it over here fast, change, get our weapons, and get them in *their* sweet clothes, and get them so they never forget it!"

The Kings cheer wildly. Gober feigns nonchalance. Only Two Heads Pigaro does not cheer. He spoils the mood with acid words. "There's a goddam rumor going round," he says, "that Babe ain't even your broad any more, Gober. If that rumor's true, I don't see no one should be insulted if Flat Head Pontiac wants to shop in a second-hand store!"

The atmosphere is tense now; you could drop a pin. The Kings watch Gober's face. His eyes needle Two Heads, but his expression remains impassive, his voice calm.

"Where'd you hear that rumor, Two Heads?"

"Around!"

"And what was that rumor?"

"That Babe ain't your cup of tea no more."

"Meaning?"

"Meaning Babe ain't your cup of tea no more."

Gober walks closer to Two Heads, slowing a foot away from him, standing and staring into Two Heads' face. "Did I refer in this meeting to the broad in question as *my* Babe, or wasn't that how I put it?"

"That was how you put it, all right," Two Heads says, "but I hear—" Two Heads stops. Gober's eyes are menacing; his breath hot in Two Heads' face. He shrugs. "Okay. So I hear wrong."

"I think you did hear wrong, Pigaro!"

"Whatsa matter? What's so wrong bringing up you're cruisin' another br—" but Pigaro does not finish. Gober's hand whips his face. Two Heads stands with his cheeks red and stinging, his eyes amazed. It is unlike Gober to work himself up over the mention of some girl. The other Kings observe the scene with the same surprise, a surprise that is tinged with uneasiness, as though they had been witness to Gober's cowardice or Gober's tears.

Perhaps the only King in the cellar who senses something familiar in Gonzalves' emotion in this interim, while Two Heads and Gober face one another, is Red Eyes de Jarro. It is the way Red Eyes feels when a King alludes to Dolores, his girl friend, whom he calls his wife; it is the kind of anger Gober has now, that stirs in Eyes when some smart King chides, "Why don't you bring this piece of yours around some time, Eyes, 'n let us inspect the goods, huh, Eyes?" So Gober has got himself hung up too, is what Red Eyes thinks; so now Gober has himself a case too.

"Geez, Gobe," Two Heads stammers, "what the hell hit you?"

"It was me that hit *you*, Pigaro," Gober answers. "I brushed a speck off your cheek. I'd be obliged you don't bring dirt into the cellar again."

"So all right. So okay, Gober," Two Heads mumbles unsurely.

"And if you want to punk out on us Friday, you go right ahead. You chicken all you want, Two Heads. You want to be a chicken, chicken!"

"I'll rumble any day of the week and twice on Sunday, and you know that," Pigaro says.

Gober says, "What's all the excitement then?"

"Yeah!" Eyes puts in. "Let's forget petty grievances and finish up this business. We got to check the arsenal anyways."

"You and me'll do that, Eyes," Gober says, turning away from Two Heads now, and resuming his earlier air. "The rest of you can quit the scene for tonight. We'll meet again for a formal pre-rumble conference on Friday afternoon. All right?"

"Right, Gobe!"

"Right!"

"S'long, Gobe, Eyes."

"Anybody going to the pool hall?"

The Kings of the Earth start for the stairs, when Gober halts them for one last piece of advice. "Want you to remember something else too," he says to them. "That is, nobody ought to walk the streets alone this week. Always at least two or three together. We don't know for sure what's on the Jungle minds. Only clue we got is they're getting goddam cocky. Might be trying to throw us off with this Friday stuff, so they can stage a jap rumble in the meantime."

"Shouldn't we carry arms, Gobe?" Bag wonders.

"Socks, maybe, knives—but nothing conspicuous. Friday we'll arm to the teeth for 'em."

"Right!"

The Kings clatter up the stone steps, shouting and laughing and pushing one another. Someone tells Two Heads he sure got Gober steamed and Two Heads answers, "Gober better not pull that again! What's eating Gober, anyway?" Braden tells Flash about the new blue lizard shoes he got and man, are they sweet; and Flash worries about the Kings being a bunch of goddam slobs compared with the Jungles. They all laugh to imagine the Jungles being surprised on Friday night when they're japped in their sugar togs; and pause under the street light at the corner as they pass by Flash, who stations himself there. Those Kings who wish to participate in the Tuesday midnight revue give their names to Flash. Blitz Giannoni tells him, "Hope she's better'n last one you lined up. Damn near fell in her!"

In the cellar Eyes and Gober examine the weapons in the arsenal, a closet they keep under lock and key. One by one they handle the heavy chains, hunting knives, switch-blade knives, hatchets, hoses, bayonets, and zip guns which are stacked there.

"Gobe?"

"Huh?"

"Dan Roan come by tonight, while Bag and me was waiting for you on the bridge."

Gober sighs. "It kills me how that guy gets wind whenever there's something brewing."

"He says he wants to talk to you before Friday."

"What's he knock himself out for, Red? You tell me that?"

Eyes shrugs. "He gets paid for it, I guess."

"You know, Eyes," Gober muses, "maybe we ought to sneak some of this stuff to the debs to carry Friday night. What you think?"

Eyes ponders this. It is safer for a gang to transport their war weapons via their girl friends, en route to battle.

A cop can search a guy, but he cannot search a girl; only a police matron can do that.

"Yeah, but it ain't like our girls are organized enough, Gobe. Take the Jungle girls. They're all organized; call themselves the Junglettes, and all. You know? They're more solid! How we know we can depend on the broads we cruise?"

"Yeah, you got a point, Eyes . . . They might let the cat outa the bag; maybe even chicken. Yeah, we better haul our own."

"The broads we cruise are nowhere, sometimes, I think, huh?" Eyes remarks.

Gober does not answer. He picks up a knife. "This needs to be sharpened," he says.

They restack the weapons silently; Gober whistling under his breath, Eyes trying to work up courage to talk something over with Gober. He manages, "Gobe?"

"Huh?"

"This thing Two Heads brought up, you know?"

"Yeah?"

"Well, for the record—I don't blame you."

"Another dull blade," Gober says, tossing a second knife aside. "I thought Braden was supposed to keep these sharp!"

"What I mean is, Gobe," Eyes continues, "sometimes a guy latches on to a broad he don't figure is anybody's goddam business."

"Okay," Gober says, "let's lock it up. Tell Braden about those knives when you see him, Eyes."

"I hope you're not sore at me, Gobe, for shooting my mouth off like this."

"Hmmm?" Gober turns the key in the lock, his back to Eyes.

"I hope you don't take offense at my discussing this with you, Gobe."

Gober turns after he has locked the closet door, and looks coolly at Red Eyes. "Did you say something, Red Eyes?"

Red Eyes gets the point. "No, Gobe," he answers, "just that Dan Roan said he wants to see you some time before Friday."

"Sure," Gonzalves says. "Detached Dan, the fix-it man. He's going to straighten us all out, huh, Eyes? Isn't that right? He's going to straighten everybody out."

"Oh boy!" Eyes howls, "how I want to be straightened out!"

The pair douse the light in the cellar and climb the steps. As they step into the night and start down 102nd toward Park, Gober says suddenly to Eyes, "This chick you keep in deep freeze, Eyes—you make out with her, or is it Emily Post?"

"She's my 'wife,' Gobe," Eyes answers in a solemn voice.

"Oh, yeah? Must be nice. Chicks like that are funny. Somehow you can't figure them from the ordinary broads."

"Dolores ain't nothing like these debs around," Eyes says. "You know?"

"Yeah."

"I mean, Gober, sometimes a guy wants something that's his, like, she moves him and all, not just a—well—" Eyes is not used to philosophical discussions with Gober; he is a little awed over the idea they are speaking to one another on such a level; a little unsure how to proceed. He tries again. "Well, like I was saying in the cellar, Gobe—"

"Yeah," Gober says, "Dan, Dan, the fix-it man, going to rehabilitate all the goddam juvenile delinquents from here to hell and back. Huh, Eyes? That's the facts, huh, Eyes?" Gober grins and clamps his arm around Red Eyes' shoulders, in a new gesture of mysterious camaraderie. "Rehabilitation blues, huh, you screw!" Gober laughs to Eyes. Eyes gives in to the new mood; the more familiar clowning mood, unfamiliar only in that Gober and he seem now to have some unnamed bond established between them. But to keep it light, to make it gay, to carry it off with the suavity expected of him, Eyes joins in on Gober's spontaneous hilarity. He croaks, "Aw hell!" and chuckling hoarsely; goes along in step with Gonzalves, singing:

> *They tried to rehabilitate me,*
> *Tried to reinstate me*
> *In the human race.*

"Oh man, are *you* a case!" Gober cries.

Together they chorus, "*I got the rehabilitation blues; the real re-ha-bil-i-ta—shun, bull-lew-oohs!*"

IV

*Let's put some teeth in the laws
dealing with juvenile delinquency!
We can start by establishing a curfew
for those under eighteen. Let them be
cleared off the streets after 10 P.M.
and in their homes where they belong!*
—GEORGE DAY, COLUMNIST FOR THE
NEW YORK BULLETIN.

AT MIDNIGHT, Red Eyes de Jarro climbs four flights up the rickety stairs of the five-story tenement on Park Avenue in the early hundreds. He opens the door and steps into the kitchen, where five of the occupants of this narrow, three-room, cold-water flat are assembled around a card table. In all, nine people live here; the Venturas, the Ricos, and Eyes and his mother.

Eyes' mother looks up from her hand of cards at him, a cigarette dangling from her red lips, her tired face cranky. In some remote way her son seems responsible for all the bad luck she has realized since Nick de Jarro deserted her, four years after Eyes was born. For one thing, Eyes closely resembles his father both in appearance and temperament; and for another, she imagines that without the burden of Eyes, she would have remarried long ago, and not have been ultimately forced to rent out her rooms in this shabby flat and work part time as a seamstress.

She says, "Where you been?"

"Out!" he answers.

"I ought to beat you in the head!" she tells him.

"Try it!"

"I'll tell your probation officer and I hope he sends you up for good!"

"Drop dead!"

This is the usual exchange between mother and son, prompted by little more than the fact that they are face to face, neither especially pleased with the other's presence. Beppo Ventura, father of Dolores, Eyes' "wife," growls, "C'mon, play your hand, Lucy! Don't waste your time on him!" Beside him, Jesus Ventura, uncle of Dolores, swigs whisky through half closed drunken eyes, and ignores Eyes' presence. Only the Ricos, a skinny couple who look remarkably like one another, grin up at Eyes over the cards they hold in their hands. It is a grin of embarrassment. They are new to these surroundings, and neither speaks English. There are perpetual fights between them and the Venturas, who must always translate for them. Now the Ricos are unsure what has been said in the interval after Eyes' arrival, and so foolishly and helplessly they smile their vague discomfort.

Eyes walks through the kitchen into the second room, and in the darkness makes his way past four mattresses strewn on the floor, more orange crates standing on their ends, and a couple of ripped plastic hassocks. He glances over at the mattress in the far corner to see if Dolores' sister, Jo, is asleep there, or out making the rounds of the bars in Spanish Harlem. Satisfied that she is out, he passes on to the last room. In this one there are only two mattresses, a metal frame bed, and an old aluminum porch swing on which Eyes sleeps.

The bed belongs to Mrs. de Jarro, and one of the mattresses to the eighty-seven-year-old grandmother of Dolores Ventura. In the dim light from the window, Eyes sees the old lady's hulking body wrapped in a blanket; moving rhythmically in the deep breathing of sound sleep. Quickly Eyes slips off his pants, under which he wears no shorts, and unbuttons his shirt and drops it on the floor beside his pants. Naked, he walks to the other mattress, slips down on it and slides under the coarse blanket. His hands curl around the lithe body of the young girl asleep there and come to rest, one on the elastic of her panties; one up under the over-sized T-shirt she wears, on her small pear-shaped breasts. His lips rub against the back of her neck longingly, and as she stirs, he caresses her gently, lovingly.

Sleepily she murmurs his name, and her hand reaches up and folds over his hand on her breast.

"You asleep, Lorry?"

"Ummm. I didn't hear you come in. I tried to stay awake."

They whisper their words softly, Eyes touching her lightly as they talk.

"You with the Kings, Dom?"

"Yeah."

"You didn't get a chance to see Mr. Roan then?"

"I saw Dan for a minute, Lorry."

"And did you show him the letter about your song?"

"I couldn't, honey. I didn't get the chance."

"You should show him, Dom. Get his opinion."

"I'm going to."

"Dom? Remember what I told you about Uncle Jesus the other night?"

"That dirty—"

"Well, tonight, Dom—just a little while ago—I was awake, and he came in here, pretending to be checking on Nanny. He came over to my bed. He was all smelly of liquor. He pulled the blanket off me and started running his hands over me, and I called Pa, but he didn't hear me, I guess. I told Uncle Jesus I was going to scream, and he said, 'I thought you were Nanny, Dolores, but you aren't Nanny at all. Why, Nanny doesn't have these! I should have known you weren't Nanny, Dolores. A thousand apologies!' And he was pinching me when he said it, and pulling at me. And when he got up he was laughing, the way he does. Dom, I was scared of him! I wanted you to be here so bad!"

Eyes curses and pulls her to him tightly. "I'll kill him, Lory! I swear to God some day I'll kill that bastard!"

"And he said to me, 'You tell your pa, little bright eyes, and I'll tell him something about you and your wop boy. I'll tell him what you and that dago do when Nanny's dreaming!' "

From the other room there is raucous laughter as Eyes curses again; and across the room from Dolores and him, the old lady begins to snore.

Tea is alone in the basement room he shares with his stepfather. It is a small, dank area squared in by plywood boards which do not reach the cellar's ceiling; and it is reached by a crooked staircase leading down from the vegetable market above it, facing Park Avenue around 99th Street. In the room there are two old iron beds, a legless glossy white bureau, and a folding chair. Salvadore Hostos, Tea's stepfather, is a night watchman for a housing

project going up on 111th Street. Tea pays him board;
$25 a month, which is what the total rent on the room is;
and which Tea earns by pushing caps for a smart money
man Tea knows only by the name Ace. With what Tea
makes from his sales of the small quantities of narcotics
Ace supplies him, he has enough left over, after giving Ace
the bulk of the profits, to support his own habit, pay
Hostos, eat, and buy sweet clothes every now and then. Tea
would just as soon cut out on Hostos as look at him, except for the fact he was paroled from Coxsack to Hostos'
care, and the fact Hostos is the only remaining tie Tea
has with any family at all. Without his stepfather to claim
him, Tea could be in a home of some kind.

It is not that Salvador Hostos and Tea Bag Perrez do
not get along. They get along. They pay no attention to
one another, so long as Tea forks over the twenty-five on
schedule. It is simply that there is a tacit understanding
between them that they dislike each other; so neither makes
the effort to pretend it is any other way. Hostos is a drunk,
a petty thief, a periodic loafer. It is beyond Tea why his
mother ever married him; save for the fact she was young,
alone in New York City, and he was the first Spanish-
speaking man she met.

From the bureau drawer, Tea takes a teaspoon, its handle
broken off, its bottom charred from the matches which
have been lighted under it. He reaches into his pocket for
a capsule, opens it and empties the white heroin into the
spoon. Then he gets a hypodermic needle and an eyedropper from the same drawer, and lays them on his bed. There
is a glass of stale water on the top of the bureau, and he
dips the spoon into it, being careful not to spill the powder.
Sitting on the bed, he strikes a match and holds the flame
under the spoon. Then with the eyedropper he sucks up the
milky fluid; next he jabs the hypodermic needle through
his trousers into his thigh. Hurrying, he puts the eyedropper
over the needle, and presses the fluid into his flesh.

"C'mon, boot!" he says to himself, grinning. "Boot up!"

Whenever Tea joy-pops he thinks of his mother, and
giggles to himself, imagining that day his mother told him
about the day she brought him to this country. Tea was
born when she was fourteen, out of wedlock, down in
Puerto Rico. His mother worked as a sugar sorter until she
saved enough for the trip to New York, made in a bucket
plane in which she stood all the way, holding Tea, then

three, in her arms. Tea likes to think about it. Tea likes to say, "bucket," when he does, and laugh. "Bucket!"

"You give me the name Tea!" Tea says to the air, remembering how his mother used to let him pick up on "pot" and call him Tea Bag, and put her arms around him and call him Bendito. He didn't even mind then when she'd kiss Hostos too; didn't even mind hearing them in the next room together, because he felt so good, so high.

"Mamita mia!" Tea titters.

For a second or so Tea's thoughts sidetrack; and he just sits rocking on the bed, singing.

"What about that day in lollypop court, boy!" Tea interrupts himself in the middle of the song. "Hey—that goddam judge!" He smiles in spite of the memory, because he feels perfect. He is remembering adolescents' court, the morning he was sentenced to Coxsackie. All that loot he stole was for her. She could sell anything he could steal, his mother. Even an old clothesline or something. She knew how to get rid of it for cash. People all liked her because she was so pretty and looked just like a girl; not like a grown woman with a kid. She was little.

"Lollypop court!" Tea repeats, "an then Coxsack U. I did it for her. She said, 'You go on out now, Tea, and see what you can find.'" Tea smiles pleasantly at the walls. "She used to be surprised at the things I could find. 'How'd you do that,' she'd say. 'Diablo!'"

Tea gets up and whistles and walks around the cellar room. He couldn't blame her for not wanting to stay with Hostos. Would he want her with Hostos if he had his way! Anyone but Hostos! She was probably with someone a whole lot better, so she doesn't have to work even. She doesn't have to steal. Wherever she is, she is better off than with Hostos. You couldn't expect her to stay with him. Tea in Coxsack and her stuck with Hostos—no! No wonder she cut out, left no word; just quit the scene. Hostos told him about it the day Tea got released. Hostos said, "What do you mean, 'Where's Ma?' I'd like to know too. She took off! Found herself someone else when you was in the clink-school. She cleared out and left her baggage behind—you!"

Tea socks the air with his fist and keeps on smiling. From somewhere far off in the distance a clock bongs one. It is good to be home. It is good to be home with the white, white, snow, for there is nothing like it.

Through a dark corridor littered with refuse, up a flight of stairs, and into the front apartment facing Park at 100th, and Gober is home.

"Riggie? Riggie?".

"Yes, Mama."

"That you, Riggie?"

"Yes, Mama."

"Come here, Riggie, talk to us. Your papa and me are in bed. What time is it?"

Gober pauses in the living room of the small two-and-a-half-room flat, and lights a cigarette. The china lamp, shaped like a heart with a gold arrow piercing its red middle, stands lighted on an end table beside the sofa upon which Gober sleeps. The room is overcrowded with big stuffed chairs, a tall old-fashioned radio and phonograph, several cotton scatter rugs, and here and there gaudy satin pillows. Wherever there is space, there are china dogs, china pitchers, glass candy dishes filled with peanuts and raisins; and on all the arms of the furniture, there are crocheted antimacassars. Banners and calendars fill the walls of the room, and the room is very clean.

"You hear, Riggie? Your papa and me are in bed. Come talk to us."

"Yes, Mama, Yes. I'm on my way there, Mama. Just lighting a cigarette."

"I wish you wouldn't smoke and ruin your lungs, Riggie. Cancer comes from those weeds. If you got to smoke, don't inhale! You don't inhale, do you, Riggie?"

Gober talks as he walks into his parents' bedroom, "No, Mama, I don't inhale."

The Gonzalves sleep in a large iron frame double bed which occupies three-quarters of the space in that small area. The rest is taken with cardboard chests of drawers lined along the wall, upon which a huge gold crucifix hangs, with an ivory figure of Christ.

"You been with your novia, Riggie? Your girl friend?"

"No. Just some of the guys, Mama."

Gober sits on the edge of the bed, in the dim light shining from a street lamp on Park Avenue. His mother is a plump woman in her forties, with black hair worn in a bun, but loosened now as she sits up in bed to talk with her son. It falls to her back, and she pulls it around her shoulders to the front of her, to cover her large breasts which show through the flimsy cotton nightgown. Beside her, lying so that he faces the wall, is her husband, George. In addition to the three of them, there are Gober's two brothers: one a Marine, the second a longshoreman, married and living off in Brooklyn with his wife and four kids. Gober is the baby. All speak Spanish when they are together.

"What's the matter with Papa? Asleep?"

"No, Rigoberto, your papa is not asleep. How is it he could sleep, hmm, Rigoberto? You tell me that." His father says this without turning away from the wall, or moving the position of his body.

"Papa don't feel happy tonight, Riggie."

"Sorry to hear that."

"Whatever you do in this life, Rigoberto, learn a trade. Learn a trade. Learn a trade. Learn a trade."

"Sure, Papa. I'll learn a trade."

"Because then you can always do something. Always. You know how to do plumbing, you always got a job. Grind lenses, set type, lay bricks—I don't care—a trade is a guarantee. A guarantee."

"Maybe tomorrow, Papa, you'll find something. Something will probably come up tomorrow."

Gober draws in on his cigarette tiredly, listening while his father turns, sits up in bed, and begins to rant. "Sure, I find something. But something is nothing. Something is running errands for a liquor store, that's what something is, or delivering for a florist—a messenger boy! Isn't that something! That's something, I'll tell you, I don't want to find it tomorrow. God, when I think! God and Mary, when I remember! When I remember how many men worked under me back in San Juan—all sugar men, all processing, and me their supervisor—and they coming to me and saying, 'I can't come tomorrow, *Mr. Gonzalves*'—mister, they'd say—'because they need us in the rum plant.' And I'd say, 'Listen, you lousy little pack rat, you come tomorrow! You come!' And they obeyed me. They obeyed my words!"

Mr. Gonzalves sits smiling wistfully to himself for a moment, nodding his head up and down, his hands clasped together peacefully. "Yes, yes," he says. "Yes, yes."

His wife consoles him. "Who knows what would be now if the market had never dropped on sugar? Who knows what would be, George?"

"What would be? I would be big! A big man! Maybe

head supervisor; maybe manager, even. Yes, manager! A manager!"

"Sure, Papa. Sure," Gober says.

"And no one would look down their nose. I would know my business. I would be in my business all my life and they would need me to tell them what to do, and they would not even let me retire, they would need me so. Not like here. 'Lie, George,' someone tells me yesterday when I go to the project to see for a job, 'Sixty is too old. They don't want a heart case.' I have to lie to them, who are no better then me. To them, who say, 'Talk more slowly. I don't understand you.' They say that to me like I'm a bug they will squash next . . . You listen to me, Rigoberto, son of my heart, learn a trade. It's the only way you will be somebody!"

"Okay, Papa. All right. Okay."

"I wished maybe Riggie would be a doctor or something professional. He goes to school, George. We never did. We don't know things except what we lived, but Riggie reads from books in school, he talks English. He talks two languages, our Riggie. Two! Fluently! Riggie, be a smart boy. Don't be dumb like Mama and Papa. It's a new world, Riggie. It's a world that belongs to the people who know things. Don't be like us. Finish school. You are smart in school. You flunked only one subject last term. Do you know how many your papa and me could pass?"

Mr. Gonzalves says, "It took more than brains at the *refineria*. A man had to be a big man inside of him, a big man to supervise. A man had to say, 'Listen, I'm boss! You do what I tell you!' He had to say it so they believed him. That's not in the books!"

Mrs. Gonzalves puts her great arms around her small-boned, short, mustached husband, drawing him to her. She slips a hand under the neck of his worn cotton nightgown, and pats his chest playfully. "You were one big cheese, weren't you, baby!" she says proudly. "I remember when I met you and listened to you talking—me, a girl of fifteen, and you in your thirties—and I thought, He's so smart! He ought to be God, or president! And I still say so!"

"Yah! Yah! Yah!" Gober's father laughs, and he ducks his head down, burying it in the immense folds of flesh at his wife's bosom.

"Don't bite!" she giggles and squeals, "Owwwww! Riggie, get this little bird off me. Oh! You crazy, crazy, crazy

—" and the pair laugh and laugh. Gober is grinning too, mildly; the cigarette burning down in his hands. He stands and watches them for a moment as they wrestle with one another in the tangled covers of the bed. Then he leaves the bedroom and walks through the living room into the tiny closet kitchen. Opening the square icebox, he studies the insides until he sees a dish of onion soup, pulls it out, and sets it aside while he plugs in the burner over which he will heat it. He stands and waits. Behind him, back in their bedroom, his parents make the noise of love; and from somewhere up above him, a radio blares a snatch of blues.

Again, she had lied to him.
She had said, "No, Pop, he wasn't in the place tonight."
"You know the one I mean?"
"I know who you mean."
"Those spics got nothing better to do than move up from Puerto Rico and go on relief! Their kids organize gangs and go out looking for people to kill. I used to think it was bad enough with the black ones living a few blocks from us —now it's worse. New York City is busting its seams with the scum of the earth!"
"All right, Pop. All right. I'm tired. I'm going to bed."
"I'd like to catch him coming around to the luncheon-ette. I'd show that brazen little bastard! Thinks he can associate with any daughter of mine! Filth!"
"Good night, Pop."
"You stay away from the likes of them, do you hear? Even in school! Keep your distance from their kind."
"All right, Pop. Good night."
In her bedroom, after she has undressed and brushed her black hair, and turned her blankets back, Anita takes the paper napkin from her pocketbook, and looks at the picture, a faint smile playing on her mouth. She tries to say the Spanish words, mispronouncing them. She whispers: *No sabe como te quiero;* puzzling over their meaning. From a popular song she had heard, she knows *yo te amo* means "I love you;" but what do these words say? *No sabe come te quiero.*
Turning the napkin over, Anita looks at the little game she had played with herself, after he had stalked out. It was a game where you wrote down two names; crossed out any letters in each which were the same; and then with the remaining letters in each, you said: "Love, marriage,

friendship, hate," in that order. Both had come out *love*.

She sits on the bed hugging her knees; remembering his eyes, how they had watched her; and how he had said her name—Nita.

Babe Limon rolls over in the narrow bed set against the wall in the one-room apartment on Madison and 106th. The red neon sign from the bar beneath her shines in, showing the shabby furnishings. Babe sighs and pushes a curler back around a lock of her hair.

"You still awake, Babe?"

Beside her, Marie Lorenzi lies, dressed in bra and panties. Babe wears a faded pink slip.

"Yeah. It's two o'clock."

"You think your old lady's coming home tonight?"

"I told you I doubt it!"

"Well, don't bite my head off. I didn't want to stay over. Could of slept at home just as well!"

"If she does come home, I can push the chairs together. . . . She won't."

"Where is she? Downstairs?"

"Who knows? Maybe at my aunt's."

"You still thinking about Gober?"

"What if I am!"

"What's so hard to forget! Cripes, I seen a million Gobers!"

"You don't know—"

"Don't know what?"

"The way Gober could be, is all."

"How could he be?"

"Well, before all this, you know? When I was first going with him he used to be special about me. Geez, I don't know, Marie. He used to call me Princess. He used to tell me I was a princess."

"Gober?"

"Yeah. I wish you knew him. I mean, I know lotsa guys, but till Gober come into my life, I never felt like anything. That's what steams me, Marie. I always felt like something because of him, and now because of how he's been acting lately, I feel like nothing. I mean, what he said about me washing my face, and the thing about the cat. Like I was nobody."

Marie leans across Babe and grabs for her package of

cigarettes on the chair, on the top of the pile of their clothing. She passes one to Babe, and they light up, blowing smoke out into the stuffy air of the room. Marie lets the cigarette dangle from her lips, and props her arms up behind her head as she lies there talking.

"How old were you the first time, Babe?"

"Twelve. Thirteen. I don't know . . . How old were you?"

"Fourteen. It happened in a line-up. Eight guys, and me howling my lungs out. S'funny, it never occurred to me it'd hurt so damn much. S'funny—even hurting like it did, I remember something that hurt a lot more that night."

"Yeah? What?"

"These guys were paying fifty cents, see. I was making four dollars. Cripes, I was so scared and just lying there wishing I was dead instead of there, and hoping it'd be over soon. This one guy looks down at me and says, 'I wouldn't pay a nickle for this piece! It's got pimples, and it's flat as I am!'" Marie exhales a cloud of smoke. "I never forgot that. I was just a kid. I didn't even know what I was doing. My brother—you know Al—he arranged it, and I couldn't believe I'd get four dollars for just letting some guys do that. And when it hurt, I thought they must be doing it wrong. But when that guy said that, I couldn't say anything back, or move, or anything. I felt like dying. That's where I got my inferior complex from."

"I'd never go in a line-up," Babe says. "Never! Not for anything!"

"I didn't even get the four bucks. Al gave me fifty cents of the money."

"Whatever made you do it?"

"Geez, Babe, you don't ask yourself that, you know? You don't ask yourself that. You're just a kid and things happen. Geez, I don't know why."

"Yeah, yeah. Things happen," Babe says. She says, "I didn't know you had an inferior complex."

"From that day on."

"Yeah?"

"I never forgot it."

Babe bends down and drops her cigarette in a half-filled cup of cold coffee on the floor beside the bed. "You ought to take some exercises—massage—you know? You can send away a quarter and get a book that tells all about it."

"I tried that." Marie Lorenzi yawns. "They don't do any good. Geez, it's ten after one. Here, put my butt out, will you? Let's get some sleep."

"Pleasant dreams!" says Babe.

"Good night," Marie answers, "Sleep tight. Don't let the bed bugs bite."

Sitting around the coffee table in the living room of the Roans' apartment up in Morningside Heights, are Dan and his wife, and the Mannerheims.

"It's one-ten," Enid Roan says. "I vote we call it a night."

"No, wait—just let me make my point, honey. Look, Nat, I'm not a fanatic. It's just that I've seen these kids—"

"Kids!" Nat Mannerheim exclaims. "Kids!"

His wife says, "Dan, Nat and I just don't have your zeal. It's a fine thing to treat youngsters individually; in fact, it's the only way they can be treated. But to expect to accomplish anything with a gang of reluctant hooligans who don't even want to be helped—I draw the line there!"

Dan Roan leans forward and knocks the dottle out of his pipe, holding it in his hand as he talks. "Martha, you and Nat are both psychologists. Child psychologists. I'm just a social worker, more or less. My only point is that all of us should work side by side to tackle this problem."

"Why, Dan? It isn't the only problem in the world. Give me a nice complicated schizophrenic child any day, but save me from a bunch of characters straight out of 'Blackboard Jungle.' I wouldn't know where to begin, and as Martha says, I don't have your zeal, so I'd probably not get anywhere. No, no, Dan—I'm a Freudian, a real party-line Freudian. One at a time, individually; analysis—that's the only answer. Otherwise you have bedlam!"

"We have it now, Nat. Have you ever seen a rumble?"

"Well, perhaps that's the answer. Remember the Malthusian theory, Dan? If the population increases more than the means of increasing subsistence does, in time many must starve, or be ill fed—or *rumble*. Rumble and finish one another off. It's not exactly the Malthusian theory, but it may be nature's way of taking care of these young hoods. They'll destroy one another in rumbles. Hmmm?"

"It's late," Enid Roan says. "Let's call it a night."

"Enid's right!" Martha Mannerheim agrees. Her husband stands up and slaps Dan Roan across the back. "Buck up, old man. You have the weight of the world on your shoulders tonight. These kids are getting you down. Why, they're probably all home right now, tucked in their beds, dreaming of zip guns." Nat Mannerheim chuckles. "To say nothing of bims, ah, Dan? Do I have the jargon right?"

"You have the jargon down pat, Nat."

"That's what would be of interest to me," Martha Mannerheim muses, "this lingo of theirs. Its origin. It would be interesting to speculate how many of those terms have oral allusions. Somebody ought to do a paper on it."

V

Walking cool is importint. For
if someone shuld walk by you cool,
and you dint know how to walk by
them cool rite back, then you wuld
be a square with sharpe corners as
wel as made fun of . . .
—FROM A COMPOSITION BY JUNIOR BROWN. AS-
SIGNED SUBJECT: "AN IMPORTANT THING TO
KNOW IN GETTING ALONG WITH PEOPLE."

WHY, GOBER WONDERS, is Flat Head Pontiac asking
for it? To walk by cool is really asking for it; and this,
added to Pontiac's promise to make the scene with Babe
on Friday night, comes out rumble. What is it that makes
the Jungle chief so rumble-hungry? Gober ponders this
as Pontiac passes him, in front of the candy store on
100th and Madison. It is four o'clock on a Monday afternoon; and Gober is standing there with Eyes, both having
just come from school.

"He's coming on like a goddam snowman, Gobe. Lookit." Eyes says under his breath.

"Yeah, I see him."

Pontiac is a six-foot, broad-shouldered, husky Italian.
He walks toward them with a slow, deliberate, panther-
like tread, chin held high, eyes half closed, head swaying
very slightly from side to side.

He takes his time. He knows what he is doing. He is
the coolest of the cool.

As he is parallel with Gonzalves, Gober sneers at him.

"How's your hammer hanging, Pontiac?"

Without looking anywhere but straight ahead, and
without batting an eyelash or moving a muscle in his
face; Pontiac says, "Heavy—but gonna be a lot lighter
Friday night, King-man."

This is the extent of their conversation; but now everything between them is spelled out unmistakably. This is

46

the engraved invitation to rumble, the real personal touch.

"Whooooo!" Eyes exclaims after Pontiac is a yard beyond them.

"Yeah," Gober answers. "He wants it real bad, all right. Well, we'll see if he's all talk and no action."

"I'm jap-happy now, if I never was, Gobe. Some gangs I wouldn't pull a jap rumble on, but the Jungles are crying for it."

"I think it wouldn't be a bad idea you and Tea mosey around and smell the wind in their turf. Be sure they don't jump us before we jump them."

"I'm thinking the same thing myself. Wonder where the hell Tea is?"

"'S Monday. I think he usually scores on Mondays. Probably sleeping under a blanket of the snow now. He in school today?"

"Yeah; left before last bell, though."

"That's where he is. Out scoring. He'll be by."

"Shall we amble on into the store, Gobe?"

"You go on in. I want to catch Nothin' Brown when he comes around."

"You gonna talk to Babe about Friday? I see her in there. Back booth. With Easy Marie."

"Yeah, I'm setting things straight with her. Probably take her over to the clubhouse."

"Atta boy!" de Jarro says.

Gonzalves stands alone then, looking up the street for a sign of Junior Brown. Under his arm, tucked in a copy of an English book, is this letter:

Dear Anita,

I'm sending this by messenger so as not to get you in trouble with your pop. I wonder if it would be possible that I could meet you after school and just talk some day??? That is all I'm interested in, to talk because we never had the chance really. I know the spot you are in with your pop, but unless I'm wrong, you do not feel the same way as he does toward me. I do not know what school you go to so you would have to let me know about this, and beside maybe you can make another sugestion about meeting me. Maybe I have got it all wrong or something stupid like that but then I can usually tell about things like this. You never said anything I know but people don't always have to say words.

Naturally I know you love me (ha! ha!) but if we could

just get together it would be nice I'm sure. What do you say about it??? My messenger will come back tomorrow for some answer. I hope you will say yes and not punk out on the deal.

Your friend Rigoberto Gonzalves.

In the distance, ambling along licking a fried chicken neck, Nothin' Brown heads for the candy store; and seeing him, Gober goes to meet him. . . .

Everybody calls the candy store Dirty Mac's; and this afternoon as Red Eyes enters, it is like all other afternoons. Everybody is there. Blitz Gianonni stands by the peanut machine; not that he would try to pinch it—he would not, though this is his specialty, swiping them and selling them to a vending machine dealer up on 125th— Blitz would not pull that on Dirty Mac. But he stands by it out of sentiment; looking at it with loving concern, because it is a very new and shiny red peanut machine, and he cannot keep from admiring it.

He is telling Braden, who stands beside him, how easy it would be to "just vamoose wid de machine. It's like nothing," he explains, fondling the little chain attaching the machine to the wall, "you spread de link wid de chisel, take de bolt out, and walk off wid de thing."

"How much you get for those, anyway?" Red Eyes asks, stepping up to the pair, looking around at the others in Mac's. Flash is in a booth with two girls, his leg up on the table, showing off his new blue lizard shoes. Two Heads Pigaro is playing the pinball, punching and jamming himself into it until the red light tells Tilt!

"How much?" Blitz says. "Fifteen dollars, usual. Can get three on a good night. The outside ones the easiest."

"You hear about D.&D., Eyes?" Braden asks.

"Uh-uh."

"He got sent off to finishing school. Came up this morning in lolly-pop court. He got sent off by that horny judge with the lisp. You know him?"

"Know him? He's the creep put me on probation!"

"Yeah?"

"Yeah. He says to me he's gonna give me a chance. He says he's got his eyes on me; I come around again, I go off to college too."

" 'At's cause you're too obvious," Gianonni says. "You

got picked up stealing, dint you? Dint you get picked up
on a fire escape wid a pipe?"

"Yeah. I was just breaking this window, you know—
cracking it with the pipe. Lady downstairs hears the noise
'n starts in screaming."

Blitz nods his head sympathetically; then he points a
finger at Red Eyes, wagging it as he talks, "Listen, next
time remember somethin'. You going to steal by breaking
in a window, you take a pillow for your tool, see? A plain
old pillow, see? Somebody see you walking along with
a pillow, they ain't gonna suspect, even going up a fire
escape. So you're going to a roof to sit and you brung a
pillow, see? Then you take this pillow and break the
window, 'n you got the sound all muffled and somethin'
to catch the glass in, see? It's a natural. Nobody gonna
suspect a guy walking along carryin' a pillow."

Red Eyes shrugs. "Ain't gonna be no next time."

"No?"

"Naw. I can't see it. Get sent to Coxsack, someplace—"

"If you're smart you don't get sent nowhere. You just
gotta be smart, Eyes."

"Naw, I got interests close to my heart to protect."

"I got those too, man, but I learn one thing this
world. Them interests get a lot more interested you, you
got a little moola to spend. You know?"

"Yeah, yeah," Eyes says unenthusiastically.

Braden grins. "Blitz, ain't you heard about old Eyes
here? He's struck oil right in his own backyard. He don't
have to cruise."

"Shove it!" Eyes snaps.

"No, I wouldn't do that," Braden interrupts. "I'm saving mine for bigger things."

The three Kings stand there like that around the peanut
machine, making small talk and yammering. Despite his
denial, what Blitz has told Eyes about the pillow interests
Eyes. Eyes needs money. He needs seventeen dollars. As
he thinks about it, his fingers unconsciously caress an
envelope he carries in the hind pocket of his trousers. Like
Gober, Eyes has a letter with him this day, a letter of
utmost importance; a letter, which like Gober's, contains
that long-shot link to some world better and bigger and
kinder. It is each boy's ace: the secret something that
holds hope, however wild and unlikely, and is too desper-

ately believed in by each to mention to another. Unlike
Gober, Eyes did not write his letter, but received it three
weeks after he had answered this advertisement in the back
pages of a comic magazine:

LYRICS WANTED!
To be set to music!
Send your lyrics today for free examination!
Be a hit writing hits!
Arco Song Writers, J. Marius Mahler, Pres.
Post Office Box 748, Chicago, Ill.

The letter was the first one Eyes had ever received
in his life; and his mother had said when she found it
in their box, "Dominic de Jarro—now who the hell is
that?"

Eyes told her, "It's your beloved sonny boy, that's who
the hell it is, and give it to me."

"I'll put a match to it, you little bastard!" she'd re-
sponded, but she had given it to him.

Eyes had read it, trembling. J. Marius Mahler, president
of the Arco Song Writers Association, assured him that
he had great promise, wanted to be the first to congratulate
him, and for an initial fee of seventeen dollars would
find the *right* arrangement for his song.

Eyes had read the letter again and again, barely able
to contain himself until Dolores Ventura had come home
from her factory job at six o'clock. The two had taken
the letter to the roof, and there sat together rereading it,
discussing it, planning and rejoicing.

"You ought to write them, Dom, and reassure them
about them being the ones that can write the music. They
sound sorta afraid you might not let them?"

"What part?"

"Here. See? They say they hope to be the lucky ones
to give you that assistance. See? Right here."

"Oh, yeah. They're the ones give me the encouragement
the first place—geez, naturally I'd let them be the ones."

"You're going to be famous, Dom."

"Geez, I don't know. S'funny, I always knew I could
write lyrics. I listen them all the time, you know?"

"And you'll get fancy and forget all about me, I bet."

"Lorry, all I want is to get us outa here. Get hitched
and just get outa here. Geez, I wouldn't forget about you.
Dint I write that song for you?"

"Seventeen dollars is a lot of money, Dom. Where you gonna get it? Dom, you gotta promise you won't—"

"Naw, Lorry. Dint I promise you I was straight now?"

"I could maybe save a little from my salary—except for Uncle Jesus. He always wants to know. He always asks and I gotta give it to him. If it wasn't for . . ."

"I'll kill him some day. If he ever touches you—"

"Maybe Mr. Roan could tell you how to get it, Dom."

"Me!" Red Eyes had exclaimed. "Me—going places!"

Standing there in Dirty Mac's, Eyes thinks back on that night. He should go and see Dan, this he knows; but he must hang around a while until Tea shows up. Tea and he have business in the Jungle turf. He can't chicken on that assignment.

"Hey, you guys see Tea?" Red Eyes says.

Blitz shrugs. "Ain't it Monday? He's probably up town trying to score."

Braden, who has been standing silently looking back at the booth where Babe Limon and Marie are sitting, says, "I think that Marie is a goddam Lesbian, way she wears them slacks alla time."

"Naw," Blitz disagrees. "It's cause her ankles is fat. She tole me that once. Comes right out wid it when I'm set to open her box. I told her if I cared what she looked like I wouldn't be there. And she bawls the whole while I'm working! Broads! Dey're nuts or somethin'!"

"Her feelings was hurt," Red Eyes says.

"She's de one brought her goddam fat ankles up. I dint!"

"You don't understand women," Braden says, "You're a slob."

"Oh, yeah, yeah. I tink I'm gonna have to unnerstand women a whole lot once I get ta be a big man. Oh, yeah, yeah, I tink so! I tink women gonna have unnerstand *me.*" Blitz slaps the side of the peanut machine. He moans, "Oh boy, how I wanna unnerstand women!"

"They're all right," Braden says.

Eyes says, "Where'd we be without them?"

One Hundred and Twenty-fifth Street bustles. People jam the sidewalks and spill out into the gutter. The afternoon is muggy and hot; but up in Harlem even muggier and hotter.

Tea Bag Perrez stands outside a record store. The music from inside is pumped through a speaker to the street. People seem to move to the music, seem to walk in beat with it, some with their feet going fast; others dragging, shaking some part of their body to it; but with it—in beat—some sitting on stools near the curb, some standing like Tea; and the music blaring out hot on a hot day, like heaping coals on a going fire; and the sweat soaking everyone. And Sara Vaughn's voice.

Tea checks the clock in the window of the café next door. Ace is half an hour late. It's not like him. Timing is everything. Didn't he teach Tea that? If you want to score, timing is everything. It only snows on time. Tea shifts the weight of his body from one foot to the other; makes time pass looking into the faces of the women, playing the game with himself. One day he is standing on a street and he sees her face suddenly in the crowd. Still young. Still pretty. Little. "Mamita mia!" "Tea Bag, my little Tea Bag. I look for you every place. Every place. Now I find you!" One day. One day he is standing there and it happens. "Mamita Mia!"

It only snows on time. Tea is jumpy; nervous. He has to figure it again. He has six caps left. Monday, Tuesday, Wednesday. If he can't score today; he can still last. Maybe Ace is hung up somewhere; maybe someone goofed, the heat is on. If it's too hot it can't snow. Still no need to get rifty. Tea can joy-pop with the caps he was going to push. Last till Thursday. No need to get rifty. C'mon Ace. *Por Dios.* C'mon Ace!

Tea waits. Three o'clock, four, and half-past. C'mon Ace. *Ratero!* C'mon ooooh, snow, Ace—snow!

In the clubhouse where Gober has brought her, Babe Limon sits on the yellow couch fumbling with the black plastic straps of her handbag. Gober leans against the brick wall, lighting a cigarette.

"You got a new card table, huh, Gober?" Babe Limon says in a voice that is uncertain and somewhat nervous. "I never saw that here."

Gober sticks his thumbs into the loops of his trousers and stares down at her, unsmiling. She wears a tight black orlon sweater under which her apple-shaped breasts swell, a black wool skirt which has lint caught over it, the same worn black patent leather pumps, and around her neck a gold chain with a cross hanging on it. Her nail polish is blood-red and chipped, and she sees Gober looking at her nails, curls them into her palms, and sits with her hands knotted into fists.

"We here to discuss card tables, or what?" Gober demands.

"I don't know. You're the one brought me here."

"Whata you jumpy about, if you don't know?"

"I'm not! Gober, you don't have the right to talk to me like this."

"You're pulling at your bag, aren't you? You're peeling all the leather crud off the strap of your bag!"

Babe's hand drops the strap and goes to the gold cross. She says, "You're not even like yourself any more. That's why."

"Meaning?"

"Meaning since you been interested in someone else, I don't get the time of day."

Gober drags on his cigarette and lets the smoke through his nose; his nostrils flaring angrily; his voice still calm; his face mean. "I want to go on record, Baby. I'm crazy to go on record. You want to hear?"

"Yes."

"I want to go on record I'm not interested in someone else. That's for the record. You get it?"

"You don't even say it nice."

"Next time I'll sing it."

"I saw you up there hanging around her, Gober. Me and Marie saw you."

"You didn't see nothing. You didn't see one thing!"

"I don't see why, if you don't—well—want *me* any more—why you don't let me off the hook, Gober."

"Because you're my girl, Baby—and there ain't a Jungle breathin' don't know it. Even Flat Head Pontiac, who ain't breathin' seeing as he's got a hole in his head the air leaks out—even he knows you're my girl!"

"Everybody knows it but me," Babe Limon says. "I'm glad the news is out. I'm going to hear it any day now."

"You don't know it, huh?" Gober walks over to her.

"No."

"You don't, huh?" He stands spread-legged, the smoke from his cigarette spiraling up past her face; his eyes fixed on her. She has her head bent, looking down at his feet, his black trousers, and his long arms dangling at his sides, his fingers with the cigarette clutched between them.

"Gober, I'm only human—a girl."

"You sure you're human, Baby. Or are you just all—"

"You talk to me in this kind of voice and expect me to know I'm your girl. Well, I don't! I'm tired of being treated like something less than the dirt on this floor!"

"You don't know it, huh?" Gober says again.

"No. No, no, no, no! I don't!"

Gober tosses the cigarette down and grinds it out with his heel. He bends over and pulls her up by her arm. Her pocketbook falls open, the contents spilling out of it. She tries to pick it up, but Gober jerks her to him. He holds her by her shoulders. "You're going to learn it," he says. "I'm going to teach you it, and you're going to learn it, and you're going to remember it!"

Gober grabs her; pulls her down with him on the couch. His mouth finds hers and he kisses her, and under him she struggles, writhes in protest while his lips still hold hers. His hands come on her sweater, yanking it out of her skirt. Then Babe Limon fights less earnestly; her movements change from the bolting, frantic ones they were, to slower, more rhythmic ones. Her smooth arm slides around Gober's back, and she pushes her lean body up against his.

He says finally, "I'm going lock the door first."

"Do you love me, Gober?"

"Sure," he says. "Sure."

He gets up and walks across the cellar, ready to slide the nail on the door, into the hole. "Get your gear off!" he tells her quietly.

She says, "You can be nice, Gobe. When you want to, you really can."

Down 102nd Street Junior Brown goes like sixty. His eyes are big as mushrooms and his face is soaked in sweat, but he stops for no one. He runs like crazy.

"Hey! Hey, where you think you're goin', Nothin' Brown," the news dealer over the Kings' clubhouse shouts as Nothin' streaks past him, "Hey, you little jigaboo, you know you ain't allowed down there! Hey, you—hey!"

Down the cement steps Junior Brown races, nearly tripping over the cartons stacked at the bottom, and reaching the door, he hears a lock being slipped into place; and he shouts, "Don't lock up, Gobe! I'm friendly. It's me,

Nothin'. I gotta tell you somethin'!" He pounds on the door. "It's me, Gobe. I gotta tell you somethin'!"

Then the lock slips back, the door opens, and Gober steps outside of the clubroom.

"Nothin' Brown, you going to get your face slammed into that wall, if this ain't damn important!"

"I swear!" Nothin' says, panting. "I swear. I run the whole way."

"Well!"

"She want see you, Gobe. She want see you."

"What! Jesus Christ, Nothin', what the hell you saying! C'mon, man, spit it out!"

" 'At's right! She want see you. She say you come the luncheonette and she talk to you. She say you come there, Gobe. She say it all right cause her old man gone be out."

"When!"

"Now, Gobe. Right now. That why I run so fast. She say you come between five 'n six and her old man be outa there, 'n it five after five right now."

But Junior Brown does not have to say it another time, for like a shot Gonzalves has taken the steps by threes. Nothin' stands before the door of the clubroom of the Kings of the Earth, where he has never been before. Inside must be wonderful things; guns and swords, secrets— all clubs have secrets—and things. Junior Brown cannot be sure exactly what kind of things, but gang things, wonderful things. He listens to hear a noise from inside; but he hears none. Eyes had told him up at Dirty Mac's that Gober was at the clubhouse. "Alone!" he had emphasized, "and he wants to stay alone! So you am-scray, Nothin' Brown. Leave Gobe be." Nothin' knew enough not to tell Eyes why he had to see Gobe. Nothin' was wised up to that deal. Now Nothin' stood on the threshold of the clubhouse of the Kings of The Earth. And Gober had not locked the door behind him. Very cautiously; very stealthily, Nothin' Brown sneaked to the door, opened it, and entered.

At first he did not see the yellow couch.

"What took you?" a voice said behind him where the couch was, "What was it took you so long? Hurry on over, hon. Your baby's waiting—all ready."

Then Nothin' Brown did see the yellow couch; and lying spread upon it Babe Limon, stark naked.

God-dog! Did he run!

VI

They tried to rehabilitate me.
Tried to reinstate me
In the human race—
Tried to civilize me
To psychoanalyze me
Man, am I a case!
—A RED EYES DE JARRO ORIGINAL.

Usually, nothing much is doing in Dan Roan's office until after ten, eleven at night. Then there is always more doing in the streets. Most of the time Dan spends working in the streets, but around seven or eight, a couple nights a week, he works at his desk, reads—maybe plays ping-pong with a kid hanging around there. His office is one of these store-front places in the early hundreds, over near Third Avenue. Besides the small, square cubicle containing his desk, bookcases, and phone, there is the larger outer area where the boys can come in any time to lounge, watch T.V., listen to the phonograph, play table tennis. It is a shabby room, the furniture either contributed to the Youth Board, or bought out of the limited funds available.

Now the place is deserted save for Dan. He sits at his desk, glancing over a postcard he received this morning from a former classmate in graduate school—Ernst Leites —a Fulbright Scholar studying in Paris. A slight sardonic grin tips Dan's lips as he reads:

Dear Dan,
Your account of life amidst the savages in the asphalt jungle was most amusing. I think you should try Paris. It is lovely now, after about ten days of appalling chilliness; really most agreeable to be here. I've been writing a paper on recent French films, and getting used to drinking wine at lunch without feeling stupefied in the afternoon, which

56

I consider a very worth-while accomplishment—the latter, not the former—heaven forbid! Any excitement in your life worth recounting? Do write.

Best, E. L.

Dan flinches suddenly at the sound of the voice behind him.

"Hi, dad, what gives?"

Turning, he sees Flat Head Pontiac leaning against the doorway, shuffling a deck of cards in his massive and well manicured square hands. Pontiac is sweet and cool; sweet in his charcoal gray trousers, tight-cut and clean; his white linen jacket; and the gleaming collar of his pink shirt set off by his narrow knitted black tie.

Dan shoves the postcard under the blotter and swings his chair around to face Pontiac. He says, "You look happy, Pontiac."

"Groovy, dad, real groovy."

"Is that so?"

"I'm on the fleece, dad."

"I didn't know you touched the stuff, Pontiac."

"Maybe you ought to make a study of the Jungles and put the Kings down. Jungles got more color to them."

"Maybe so. Sit down?" Dan watches as Pontiac eases himself down into a plastic-covered armchair beside his desk. Pontiac looks around the small office, still shuffling the cards, his long legs sprawled in front of him. "This is a real gas, dad, this place. This is Endsville, dad."

"It's okay, I guess."

"Not much business tonight."

"Not much."

"Too bad. Jungles would keep you busy. Kings are dead heads."

"You just on a social call, Pontiac, or you have something on your mind?"

"Social, dad. Just getting to know my neighbors better. A kind of good-neighbor policy."

"Fine."

"Groovy, huh? Never been in this place. Always wondered about it. Used to think, *man*—those Kings must be big men to have their own special social worker assigned just to study them. Big men! I used to think that. Maybe my opinion's changing. I don't know. What do you think, dad?"

Dan lit a cigarette and offered one from his pack to
Pontiac, who took it, inspected it, handed it back. "I only
smoke filter tips, dad. Don't want to get hung with
the cancer kick."

"Horse doesn't improve your health either, does it?"

"It doesn't give you cancer, dad."

"Dan's the name, Pontiac."

"So maybe I miss my old man or something, dad. You
know I saw him last time when I was pushing nine.
Haven't seen him since."

"Um?"

"He's a four-time loser, cooling his heels up in a place
called Pontiac. That's why I took the name Pontiac.
Sounds like home. You know the song? Be it ever so
humble, there's no place like prison." For the first time
Flat Head smiles; then guffaws. Dan sits smoking, letting
him play it his way. "Yeah," Pontiac continues, "he was
a real creep, my old man. You psychologists got a better
word for creep, dad?"

"I'm not a psychologist."

"No? I heard you was Sigmun Frewd."

"Sorry."

"That's okay, dad. Don't let it get you. Yep, you
definitely bring back memories of my old man. You know
something, dad? You know one day he come home, see—
we had a nice home—see? Well, on this particular day
I'm stretched out in front of a roaring fire, just sort of
relaxing like, see? An the old man, he just come in
the door and beat me silly. He was a very sick man."

"Sounds sick."

"Just because we didn't have no fireplace. He gets all
burned up. That's sick, isn't it, dad?" Pontiac's sides
shake with laughter at his own joke. Dan smiles grimly.

"My mother though, dad, she's a gas. Real groovy, my
mother."

"Ummm."

"You see she was always a couple years older than the
old man. She was smarter than him, probably because
she was older. You know, my mother, dad—we're celebrat-
ing her ninety-ninth birthday come Sunday. Imagine that,
dad?"

"Congratulate her for me, Pontiac."

"Oh, she won't be in on the celebration, dad. She come
down with a cure there wasn't any disease for when she

was twenty-nine. Went just like that—" Pontiac snaps his fingers, all the time grinning and guffawing.

"Okay, Pontiac," Dan says, "your routine's real groovy. Now, what's the point?"

Pontiac sits solemnly for a few moments, shuffling the deck of cards in his hand, looking at them through his narrowed eyes. Finally, still with his eyes on the cards, he says, "The Jungles feelings are hurt, dad. The Jungles wonder why no worker been assigned to study them, dad."

"I gathered that, Pontiac. What do you want me to do about it?"

"Well, that's what we figure. We figure there's not too much you can do, dad. We know you're not the boss man or anything. So we're going to sort of put things in motion on our own, dad."

"Look, Pontiac, for your information, the Youth Board is sending you a worker in a month or so."

"Not soon enough, dad. Not nearly soon enough. We got a rep to consider. Of course, we're not as big a gang as the Kings, but we're tougher. We're going to prove that, dad."

Dan puts his cigarette out in the glass ashtray on his desk, and leans forward. "You mean this rumble coming up is all because the Jungles don't have a worker assigned them?"

"That's one gripe, dad. All the tough gangs got workers assigned them."

"And if you got a worker assigned you tomorrow, then you'd call the rumble off?"

"Dad, you're real crazy the way you come on. Dad, you don't get the picture. It's too late now, dad. We put the seeds down for a rumble and they're going to grow. We don't chicken, dad. There's not a Jungle punk in the lot of us. We got plans. You should know our plans. We got ways and means of breaking up that whole pack of Kings; maybe even sort of absorbing them, dad."

Dan sighs and leans back in his chair; he picks a pencil off his desk and plays with it as he talks. "So what you're here to say is that there's no way to stop this rumble?"

"You're in Correctsville now, dad."

"That's your whole point, Pontiac?"

"That's my whole point, dad."

"Just to say you're going to rumble, come hell or high water."

"Just to tell you, dad, that it's too late. Maybe you pass the information on to those ass-high boss men of yours and it won't come off like this again."

"And what are you going to gain from it, Pontiac? A shiv in your side? A rock in your head? A vacation up the river?" Dan tosses the pencil down disgustedly. "What are you going to gain from it, you and the other Jungles?"

Pontiac stands up. He tosses the cards into the air in a straight row; catches them with his hand, and snaps them into his palm smartly. He grins at Dan Roan. "I'm going to be promoted, dad. From pupil to teacher. That's groovy, dad, you dig me? I'm going to teach a bunch of joe colleges a course in juvenile delinquency; its causes and cures, dad. Isn't that a gas?"

"Then Babe Limon really hasn't very much to do with it?"

"She is the means by which I reach my end, dad."

"And just suppose, Pontiac, that Gonzalves no longer goes with Babe?"

"Come off it, dad. You know the rules of the game. Technically she is his chick. Everybody knows that, dad. After I make my play for his broad, a rumble is inevitable. You like that big word?"

"It's swell, Pontiac."

"I thought you'd flip over a big word like that. Look, dad, the votes are in, see. It's in the cards. If the Kings chicken, it'll be the chicken of all chickens."

Pontiac lingers momentarily, flipping the cards from one hand to another, leaning in the doorway.

"Good-by, Pontiac," Dan Roan says emphatically.

Pontiac starts to go. He pauses halfway out, turns, and smirks at Roan. "You know, dad, you're a *sick* man! I could tell the way you just said good-by. Yes sir, dad. You're a very sick man."

Pontiac quits the scene then; sweet and cool as when he arrived.

Coming down 106th Street at eight o'clock that Monday evening are Tea and Eyes. Before they notice the car which is parked up in front of the Youth Board, they talk. Because it is a sticky night, neither wears the black leather jacket of the Kings, but instead, white T-shirts, stamped with crowns; garrison belts with two small gold crowns affixed to them; levis that hang just

below their bellies and turn in tight, hugging their
ankles; soiled sneaks and sweat socks. This is the informal street attire the Kings favor. Eyes, taller than
Tea, looks down at him as they walk; and the two
pass lazy tenants of the dilapidated apartment buildings
lounging on their doorsteps, fanning themselves, reading, staring, chatting, and kids playing stick ball in the
streets; girls in groups, their faces made up freshly, their
eyes interested in Eyes and Tea, their laughter high-
pitched, their Spanish, fast and soft, like a buzzing sound.
And there's a cop or two pacing with his night stick
swinging, and storekeepers in white aprons standing out
front to escape the flies inside.

Eyes is saying, ". . . so I smelled around in Jungle
turf solo, Tea, because you didn't show at Dirty Mac's,
and Gober said we should case them."

"I was trying to score. I still got a lead where I might
yet. I think the heat's on Ace. If so, I feel a foul-up
coming on. Man, like, I can't goof on the hopheads that
depend on me for their snow. I gotta deliver—and take
care of me too."

"You sure are a cat who really loves to boot up, Tea."

Tea shakes his head and rubs his arms where there
are marks of popping for joy. "Yeah, yeah," he agrees;
"*si, si.* So what'd you find out from Jungle land?"

"They're going to play the rumble by the rules. They
don't figure we'll jap them; they figure on Saturday
night. Pontiac plans to tell Gobe, after he's come on with
Babe, 'If you don't like it, show up with your punks
Saturday night at Park, in the lot there.' "

"Who told you this, Eyes?"

"A very reliable source. You know their lookout, Silly
Charlie?"

"Sure, he's a stupido. A moron."

"Yeah. Well, he doesn't like the fact they make him
lookout, see? And don't let him in on all their doings, see?
So I told him he could be a scout for us, and we'd take
him into the Kings as a War Counselor if he proved
himself."

"That's good tactics, Eyes. Gotta hand it to you."

"He says Pontiac figures Gober would never jap, because Gober is so straight, you know? Like, Gobe don't
steal or get with the rackets much, so he figures Gober
ain't the kind would jap. Besides, Pontiac wants a big

show, see? And if you jap, he figures, you can't always have a big show, see? You know, you surprise a bunch and there might not be much but a—"

"Hey, amigo—lookit! Lookit up ahead!"

Eyes and Tea stop dead in their tracks and stare at the shiny new Buick convertible parked in front of Dan's offices. It is powder-blue, and hanging from the radio aerial is a mink tail with a red ribbon around it. It is sleek and full of chromium; and behind the wheel is Flat Head Pontiac, smoking a cigarette out of an extra-long powder-blue holder. He has the radio turned on and up, and he is just sitting there like that, looking very much like a very big man, a smart money man.

"Idioto!" Tea says. "Ratero!"

Eyes says, "Jesus Christ!"

The pair continue on their way now, walking toward the car, making only inane conversation between them, and cursing, and watching Flat Head.

"I hear that ain't even his car," Eyes says. "I got the news was his brother's car, on loan while he does time up in Auburn."

"His whole family's in the clink, I hear," Perrez says.

"Where else you gonna keep 'em, make society safe?"

"Could bury 'em," Tea says.

As they come alongside the Buick, neither Tea nor Eyes looks at Flat Head. They pause before the Youth Board.

"You going to see Detached Dan, ah?"

"Yeah. You coming?"

"Naw, I gotta lead on Wintersville. Gotta case it for snow. I'm really rifty about why Ace never showed."

"Then I see you around tomorrow. School."

"Yeah."

Just as they salute and start away from one another, Pontiac halts them, by yelling at Tea, "Hey, Perrez. What's a matter, Perrez? You look pale or something."

Eyes and Tea give him a cool look.

"You didn't make your connection with Ace today, did you, dad? That why you're caving in in the middle?"

Tea shouts, *"Besame el culo!"*

"Kiss mine!" Pontiac laughs back.

Tea shouts the vilest of Spanish oaths. Cool as he is, Pontiac steams when he hears it. His face flames in anger. "You're going to see, dad. Wait until you want a flake from the tall white horse, dad. I dig spic talk, dad."

"*Ah, besame el culo!*" Tea repeats again.

Pontiac turns his key in the ignition, the cigarette holder between his teeth, clamped by angry jaws. He guns his motor. He backs his Buick into the truck parked behind him, lets it ram it, and then gives it the gas, swings the wheel furiously, and takes off.

Tea yells an obscenity after him, and Eyes stands laughing.

Once Pontiac is out of sight, Eyes says, "That's laying it on him, Tea Bag! Did he cut out!"

"Yah! Yah! He's all talk and no action."

"Take it easy," Eyes waves as he turns in at the Youth Board.

"It isn't hard," Tea grins.

After Dan Roan has read the letter Red Eyes handed him, he puts it down on his desk, rubs his eyes, thinking, and sighs. A few boys have wandered into the room outside his office, and he hears the noise of the ping-pong balls being hit across the wooden table, the phonograph blaring, and the sound of the boys' gruff voices intruding on the still interior.

Sitting on the edge of his seat, Eyes searches Dan's face anxiously. "Of course I don't know where I'm going to get seventeen dollars, Dan, that's the only thing. I mean, I just don't have that kind of money."

Dan nods. "Umm," he says, meditating.

"It's a swell letter, isn't it? Geez, I never even got a letter before, and this one's swell."

"They don't mention the title of your song in the letter, Red Eyes. Is it one I know?"

"I don't think I ever sung it for you, Dan. It's a recent one. I mean, it's serious, you know?"

"You want to sing it?"

Eyes glances at the open door nervously, and Dan stands, pushes it to, and sits back again in his chair. "Go ahead," he says.

Whenever Eyes sings a song he has written, he sings it on his feet, in a rigid posture, with his hands at his sides. Invariably, his face reddens, and he cannot look anywhere but at the floor.

He mumbles, "It's called *I've Got Some News.*"

He waits a moment, shuffles his feet, draws a breath, and then sings his song.

I've got some news for you
I cruise just you
I flip more than on booze for you

Your lips are the sweetest lips
I've ever tasted
For your lips, for your kiss,
I'd even get wasted.
I'd take a lickin', dear
I'd chicken, dear
I'd punk out without any fear
If you would only say "I do"
I'd do anything you wanted me to . . .

I've got some news for you
I cruise just you
I even sing the blues for you . . .

So say okay, say sure, say yes,
Say by the way, I too confess
I've got some news for you. . . .

When Eyes is finished he slumps down in the armchair opposite Dan and blushes, and pulls at his nails, not looking up at Dan.

Dan says, "It's a good song."

"Geez, thanks, Dan! Course, you understand the music I sung to the words ain't going to be the music. I mean, the music I sung is just stuff I put to the words myself. That's why I need the seventeen. To get some real classy melody to the words. I'm strictly a words man, you know? A lyricist."

Dan doesn't say anything for a while and it makes Eyes uncomfortable. He says, "I thought maybe even I'd take a job or somethin'. Earn the moola I need. You think I could take a job, Dan?"

"I'm sure of that."

"You think that's the best idea?"

"I think it's a swell idea for you to take a job. Not just for this, but because you'd earn yourself quite a bit, be sort of free from dependence on home."

"Home! For Chrissake, only money I get from home, I get takin'."

"How do you have any to spend, Red Eyes?"

"Lorry—I mentioned her before—she gives me a little now and then from what she earns, but not much. And I don't like to take it from her!" Eyes says emphatically.

"So?"

Eyes shrugs. "So I do errands for the numbers boys, or pick up a little here and there. Nothin' really against the law, you know? Small time stuff, just like all the other guys."

"Well, I think a job would be swell. I'll start working on one for you."

"When I get seventeen dollars, I quit. I'll make big money then. Geez, these songs make a lota moola, Dan. Records, and all."

Dan stands up and walks to the window, his fists leaning on the sills. The scene outside is backyards of tenements; and smoke from trash fires. He says, "Eyes?"

"Yeah?"

"You want me to give it to you straight?"

"Sure, Dan, only no preaching."

"No, I'm not going to preach. I'm just going to explain something to you."

"Go right ahead."

Dan turns and faces de Jarro, who stares up at him blankly.

"This letter, Eyes—this alleged song-publishing house— it's a racket. It's a racket aimed at getting money out of you. No matter who sent a song poem in to them, no matter what the lyrics were, a letter like this would be sent out."

For a moment, Red Eyes cannot comprehend what Dan has told him.

"It's a racket," Dan continues, "and nothing more. Sure, they'll put music to your song—after you've invested enough so they can make a profit. But your chances of ever getting that song before the public eye are almost nil. I hate to take the wind out of your sails, but those are the facts."

Eyes argues, "How can they advertize a racket in a magazine, for Chrissake? I seen this right in a magazine."

"Just take my word for it—they can. It's a more subtle racket than the numbers or the horses, but it's crooked just the same."

"Then you mean—" Red Eyes' voice trails off.

"I mean you've been taken, Eyes, plain and simple.

You've been taken in—but luckily you didn't lose any money."

"You sure, Dan?"

"Positive."

"Yeah? Geez."

Eyes sits dolefully, playing with his hands, his head bent. Dan walks over to the desk, folds the letter and puts it back in the envelope, and hands it over.

Eyes pushes his hand away. "I don't want it!" he snaps.

Dan says, "At least you've learned about another racket, Eyes. That's something."

Eyes is not listening to him. He is thinking his own private thoughts. Finally, he says, "You said my song was good."

"It is good."

"Well, maybe—maybe you could find some way I could get a melody set to it and get it published. You do that, Dan?"

"Number one, Eyes, I don't have those kind of connections. And number two—well, I'm going to give it to you straight again. The song's good, but it's too limited. The words you use, for instance—people don't know them."

Eyes grumbles, "So I suppose they know words like 'ko-ko-mo, I love you so.' You ever heard that? Hell, I don't even know what ko-ko-mo means. People don't have to understand the words!"

Dan grins. "Well, you've got a point there."

"Sure! Who needs to know the words? Besides, everyone would catch on to what I mean. What's so difficult?"

"How many people know what 'to get wasted' means?"

"Who don't, for Chrissake? Everyone in New York City knows, anyway, and New York's biggest city in the world!"

"After London."

"New York's bigger 'n London! What are you, wise? It's the biggest city in the world! And ask anyone in New York what it is to get wasted. They tell you."

"I doubt it, Red Eyes. You forget New York extends below East Ninety-seventh for quite a way, and beyond that, west, south, and north. It's not all the same."

"Geez! Who needs a geography lesson!" Eyes gets up abruptly. "Okay, Dan," he says, "so you don't like my song. So you're not with it. The Kings will sure be interested in this news, Detached Dan."

"I hurt your feelings, so you threaten me. Is that it?" Dan scratches a match to light a cigarette. "I thought I could talk to you like a man, and that you could take it straight."

"So what the hell!" Eyes stands sullenly; ashamed now of his behavior.

For a moment Dan Roan smokes silently, watching him without saying anything. Finally he swings his chair back to his desk, opens a drawer, takes papers from it and begins to work on them. Eyes moves slowly to the door. As his hand turns the knob, Dan says without looking up, "By the way, Eyes, you were going to let me know about Thursday night."

Eyes tells him, "I ain't made my mind up yet."

"Well make it up—right now!" Dan says.

Eyes opens the door. Before he steps out of Dan's office he mutters, "Okay. I'll go to the goddam show. I'll do you the favor. Can't kill me!"

VII

A prerequisite to the understanding of the causation factor in delinquency is the acceptance of the fact that instincts inevitably strive for satisfaction whether socially acceptable or not. The instinctive urges of the juvenile delinquent are no different in this respect from the impulses of the law-abiding juvenile. It is the ego which decides which impulses may become overt, and the ego is guided in this decision by the demands of reality, and by the voice of the superego. The ego of the juvenile delinquent is still governed by the pleasure-principle, i.e., as a prerequisite to . . .
—FROM "ANTISOCIAL CAUSATION CLARIFIED," PSYCHIATRIC BULLETIN, VOL. VII.

UP IN CENTRAL PARK there is a spot called Harlem Mere. You can sit on a bank up there under the trees on a hot afternoon, and if there is a breeze, you can feel it cool on your face; and if there isn't, you can watch the lake water and imagine how it feels, and lean back, and pull up some grass, just wet from being hosed, and watch the rowboats bobbing on the lake. If it is a nice day, like this Tuesday afternoon, close to four, you can look up through green leaves and bark boughs and see the sky, all that blue and those clouds, and it isn't bad at all—for New York near Harlem. It is as good a place as any to loaf around and talk with someone you like.

". . . I mean, to hear it told, Nita, you'd think just because a guy belongs to a gang he's some kind of hood, runs around cutting people up no reason. You know?"

Anita Manzi sits beside Gober, her raven-colored hair loose at her shoulders and falling on the white bareness of her skin. She wears a simple yellow dress which dips down her back, and in the front forms a V-neckline. She wears a thin strand of pearls, she is barelegged, and on her feet she wears rope sandals that tie around her ankles.

Gober wears the Kings' T-shirt, khaki pants, and sneaks without socks. Around his waist is the King garrison belt.

She says, "I just don't see why you have to belong to a gang."

"I don't have to. I can be a creep, if I want to."

"My brother doesn't belong to any gang. My brother Al. He's your age. And my brother Bob didn't when he was your age. He's going to be a doctor now. He's swell, Gober. I wish you could meet him."

"You talk like I never met anybody but the gang. I got a family too, you know. Brother in the Marines. Brother in business. Both highly respectable."

"I didn't mean anything by it, Gober. I just meant I wish you could meet Bob."

"So maybe I will."

"I told him about you, Gober. I tell him things I wouldn't tell anyone else."

"Don't tell me someone in your family approves of me?"

"Well—" Anita pauses, picks a blade of grass and sucks on it. "I just wish you didn't have to be a King."

"Look, Nita," Gober says, "I don't know nothing about where you live—up on Ninety-fifth Street. We live only a few blocks from each other, but I don't know nothing about your street. It's the difference between two worlds. I think about that sometimes. I even figured out just when the difference begins. I figured out it's got to do with the trains. You know all the way on up to where I live, they run underground, and all their soot and dirt stays under the earth. But just when they get right to where I live, those trains come shooting up out of the ground and run in the open; and they spit all over me, and people 'at live where I do. And that's the difference. The trains run in the open in places where it doesn't matter a damn 'bout the people there!"

A plane roars overhead, and three little Negro kids with sticks climb down a bank opposite Gonzalves and Anita, singing, *"Davy, Davy Crockett!"* Anita touches Gober's wrist with her long fingers, very lightly, saying nothing, but watching his petulant profile.

"And that's what I mean, I guess," Gober continues. "We don't live in the same world. If this was one of those soap-box operas, you'd be a rich dame on Park Avenue or something, and I'd be a nothing. But you're not rich, and I'm not nothing. I'm a gang leader. They don't just grow on trees. You don't just get born one. And maybe the Kings aren't angels—maybe not—but they stick together, and nobody puts anything over on them."

Gober looks down at her then, at her eyes, and at her hand on his wrist. He murmurs, "Don't you see, Nita?"

"But if you didn't belong to a gang," she says quietly, "then maybe we wouldn't have to sneak around to see each other and—well, you know, Gober. If you—"

"Yeah," Gober groans, "if I didn't belong to a gang. If I didn't live on the wrong side of the street. If I wasn't a spic—"

"Don't say that, please."

"Well, I *am* a spic. What the hell!"

"You say it as though it was something bad to be, and that's why it's all right for you to lead a gang and have those wars and all."

"Wars are the least of it! What do you think, it's all rumbles?"

"I don't know what it is. It's something I don't know about. Neither of my brothers ever had to be in a gang. Bob's going to be a doctor and Al's going to take over the luncheonette some day."

"Okay," Gober says. "So I don't have any luncheonette to take over. So I don't have the brains to be no doctor."

"You're smart, Gober. You are! I know that."

Gober laughs and presses her hand in his. He says, "Oh, boy, am I smart!" and they sit there holding hands, the muggy May air pressing in on them. They sit watching the scene before them. There are others in Harlem Mere sitting just like Gonzalves and Anita, or walking along leisurely, or lying with half their bodies exposed to the sun, spread out on the grass, or just standing around doing nothing. They watch and keep their hands in one another's; and after a while, in a low, steady voice, Gober starts to talk.

"I'm smart, all right. You should see my grades. You should see everything said in school just going right over my head. What do I know?" He laughs. "My mama, she tells me, 'Be good, Riggie, finish school, Riggie. Don't be like us, your pa and me. Look where we are today. Get an education, Riggie. Be smart. Don't be like us.' Well, I am like them! I'm their kid, and I'm like them! I know I am! Every time in geometry, English, science, I get an assignment, I know I'm dumb—real dumb. I don't have the sense to learn. I'm like my ma, who can't even learn any English, cause she just don't know how. I'm like that. And you know something else?"

"What?"

"Ever go inta one of these drug stores, see the quarter novels there?"

"Yeah?"

"Well, they got this novel called "Anybody's My Name." That's the title. I seen it lotsa times. Well, it just makes me say to myself, 'Anybody ain't *my* name. My name's *somebody*.' See? I don't wanta be *anybody*. Even a big fish in a little river is better, see? That's my papa in me. That's how he is. He lives in the past when he was heading a whole crew of workers, back home in the *refineria*, processing sugar. My papa lives back there when he was somebody, cause he don't want to be *anybody* either. And I'm his son, his flesh. I'm the King of Kings, Nita, can't you see that?"

"Gober, Gober—I don't know what to say when you talk like that. I want to cry or something."

Gober says, "I want you to know the way it is with me, that's all. I don't want to fool you, Nita."

"I know, Gobe," she says softly, squeezing her hand inside his.

"I'm no hood, but I'm no doctor. My family don't know much up in this country, but they did. My mama used to dress swell—like you. We're not spics. We're Puerto Ricans come here because we're citizens here. We're citizens here! My mama and papa got as much right here as yours—"

"Mine immigrated here, Gobe, too," Anita says, smiling up at him. "They had to wait to become citizens. I'd like your folks. I would, Gobe."

"You want to meet them?"

"When?"

"Right now! Right now! We'll go over right now and you can meet them!"

Anita glances at the cheap gold watch on her wrist. She bites her lips and shakes her head. "I can't. I have to be at work in a half an hour."

"Then tomorrow!" Gober is insistent. "This time tomorrow!" His voice still contains a note of angry resentment, and a hint of his belief that he will be rejected by Anita Manzi.

Instead, he hears her say, "All right, Gober. Sure! Sure, I'd like that."

"You would?" He looks at her with incredulousness.

"Yes, Gober. Yes." She smiles at him; and there is something about her eyes that is beautiful, that Gober memorizes, that quiets him, makes him feel peace. Gober grins down at her. "I've never brought an *amante* home before," he tells her.

"An *amante?*"

"You know—a—" Gober is embarrassed, "a girl friend." He says the last words very fast, and looks away from her.

"Really, Gober?"

"Never!"

"Will it be all right?"

"Sure," he says happily, "sure it will. Mama will be surprised!" He chuckles, tossing his head back, a lock of his black hair falling on his forehead. "Mama will think I must have got you pregnant," he laughs. "Mama will think we must be going to have to hitch up!"

High up in a duplex overlooking Fifth Avenue, Nothin' Brown stands in Mr. Morganhotter's bedroom. He has been sent up there by his mother to pack in the laundry bag all of Mr. Morganhotter's dirty shirts, and he is taking his time carrying out this order, for he knows the Morganhotters have hot-foot it off to abroad on the *Queen Elizabeth* last week.

Nothin' ambles over to the bureau and sets on top of the glass there the tomato he has been chewing. Then he walks around and around, saying to himself, "Man oh man this here is the berries; this here is big man's turf, and that's a fact!"

Nothin' sees a cane in a stand full of canes, pulls it out and gives it a twirl, and struts and giggles, and raps an end table with it. "Atten'shun, Kings of the Earth!" he says. "I'm a gonna call this here meetin' in orders. And first things on the agenda first."

Nothin' strolls smartly across to a chaise longue and picks a silk necktie off the arm; he puts it around his neck. Then he sees a Homberg on a velvet-covered chair near the bed; this he slaps on the back of his head, still twirling the cane. He saunters in a circle and stops before a full-length mirror, pointing the cane at himself.

"On the agenda first," he says, "is the fact since I become a big man, you Kings been cruisin' me to join your old gang. Well, as you know, I put you down every time, and I don't have to spell that out for you. On the agenda second," he says, "is the fact that Gober, King of Kings, been taken sick and his sickness got to do wid the fact that I put you down, and Gobe always been my bestest fren, and I don't want nothin' to happen him. On the agenda third—" Nothin' taps his cane three times on the floor—"is a fact I agree to join this here Kings of the Earth gang, and that's a fact."

Nothin' Brown smiles and bows to the applause he hears ringing in his ears.

"And now, Kings," he says, "I got cut out on you cause I got an appointment—"

"You got an appointment, all right, Junior Brown!" a voice shouts behind Nothin'. "You got an appointment wid de back of dis brush on the back of your be-hind, Junior Brown!"

Nothin' jumps when he sees his mother. She looms toward him like a giantess, a hairbrush in her hand. "Lookit your greasy hands on Mr. Morganhotter clothes! You got appointment, all right, Junior Brown. You gonna meet wid it right now!"

"You don't have spell that out for me," Nothin' says, "Noooo, ma'am!"

And dropping the cane, Nothin' bolts past his mother, out the room, pausing only long enough to grab his tomato off Mr. Morganhotter's bureau.

Goddam, Tea thinks, that idiot preacher got a prayer meeting every night the week! Tea stands before the storefront church on 116th Street. In the window is a crudely painted sign:

RONE'S ROAD TO HEAVEN.
COME IN AND GET ON THE RIGHT TRACK.
HEAVEN IS GRANDER THAN NEW YORK,
AND IT IS GRANDER THAN RICHMOND,
CHARLESTON, OR NEW ORLEANS.
IT IS SO GRAND!
ITS STREETS ARE GOLD!

Tea looks at the clock in the window of the church, a big round one with blue lights and gold hands, telling eight o'clock now.

From inside the church a chorus of lusty voices are singing:

> *No, I don't care,*
> *No, I don't care,*
> *Don't care where you bury my body*
> *My little soul gwine rise and shine!*

Service going to last another hour, Tea bets. Can't hang around out front. Draw attention. Go on inside and sweat it out. Jesus! Tea walks through the door, past the preacher's sitting room with its stuffed divans, camp chairs, and walls covered with plastic crosses and more hand-painted signs:

> JESUS, I GOT MY TICKET FOR THE TRAIN!
> LORD, HEAR ME WHEN I SING!
> HEAVEN IS MY HOME, LORD, TAKE ME THERE!

At the entrance to the next room, the room of God, there is a black curtain pulled to. Where the curtain meets the dirty floor, there is painted in faded gold letters: YES, YOU ARE ON YOUR WAY TO HEAVEN! Tea goes in to heaven.

Heaven is a large, square room with red satin curtains hanging ceiling to floor, all the way around. Chairs placed in rows face the front where stands a wooden platform, shaped like a half-moon and covered with yellow satin. On the platform is a cylindrical pulpit, painted black, with the words JESUS SAVES written across it in gold. Preacher Rone, a giant-sized, dark-skinned Negro, wearing a robe cut from the same satin as the curtains, and with a gold monk's cap on his head, leads the singing in heaven, stomping out the time with beats on the platform. A couple dozen members of heaven rock in their seats and cry out the song:

> *When I git to heaven,*
> *Gwine ease, ease,*
> *Me and my Lord goin' do as we please*
> *Sittin' down side of the lamb!*

Tea stands in the back of heaven, under the big black wire fan blowing warm air around the room.

Preacher Rone shouts, "Where you wanna go?"

The congregation calls back to him, "Heaven, Lord! Heaven!"

The preacher slaps his hands and sings:

> *I wants to go to heaven* (slap, slap)
> *Have some angel wing* (slap, slap, slap)

The congregation bursts out: "See de King Jesus—De Jesus King—"

"And do what?" Preacher Rone shouts.

"Do what de angels do, Lord!" is chorused back.

Preacher Rone says, "Sing it!"

> *Shout like de angels shout*
> *Set in de angels seat*
> *Eat what de angels eat. . . .*

Tea moves over to a bench in a corner under the fan and sits wiping his perspiring face. Song after song he sits through. Heaven is busting its gut tonight! Everyone got to say a prayer himself, standing up while the rest clap and inject "Yes, Lord;" "Tell the Lord;" "You know, you know;" "That's true, Lord, hear him!" Tea tries to sleep, but can't. He thinks: Preacher got a good racket. Used to be subway conductor, then decide to be preacher. People believe anything, you put God on the end of it.

> "And the Lord—"
> *"Oh, yes—"*
> "He say—"
> *"He said it—"*
> "Ha! Gwine be—"
> *"Tell it!"*
> "A judgment day!"

Gets hotter and louder in heaven. Some heaven! Can't hear yourself think, f'Chrissake. Everybody livin' it up. Gettin' with it. Flippin' all over the place. Preacher doin' all right. Pass the hat between sets. Give him the bread money cause he say he God.

"Tomorrow night!"
"Tomorrow night!"
"Ain't gwine sin!"
"Ain't gwine sin!"
"Gwine come right in!"
"Gwine come right in!"
"Into my heaven!"
"Into my heaven!"
"Round half-past seven!"
"Round half-past seven!"

This is the windup for the last pitch. Tea is soaking with sweat. Lord, that preacher won't ever come off it, even when he's building down. Eight-forty-five. Still all stomping their feet. God, God!

Heaven is breaking up at last, people filing out. Some stragglers lag to tell the preacher their problems. "Bring 'em to the Lord," he says.

"You convinced me tonight, Preacher Rone. Ain't never gonna steal no more."

"Stay convinced, brother!"

"You sure set me on fire, Preacher!"

"Was the warm breath of Jesus, sister, breathing down your spine."

"You had the word, Preacher."

"I heard it from the Lord hisself!"

At last Preacher Rone sees Tea, in back the church. He frowns. What the hell! Tea looks him in the eye and raises an eyebrow. The preacher gets short with his flock, and tells them he'll see them tomorrow night, right here in heaven.

Tea doesn't move until the place is cleared except for the preacher. Then he walks over to him, over near the exit from heaven, where the preacher is closing the curtain after the congregation.

Tea says, "I come here because I want it to snow, Preacher. It didn't snow for two days."

The preacher turns, pulling the robe off his big body. "The chicken alights on a rope," he says matter-of-factly. "The rope doesn't get any rest and the chicken doesn't get any rest."

"Never mind the double-talk. You can make it snow. Don't tell me you don't have none. All I want is some for me and enough for the hopheads I supply until I get the word on Ace. You can have a cut on the pushing."

"The world is in a bad way," Preacher Rone says, folding his robe over his arm carefully, "when an egg falls and breaks the bowl."

"Stop beatin' your gums!" Tea snarls. "I don't know what the Christ all that gum-beatin' means!"

The preacher puts his robe over the back of a chair. Then he turns and looks down at Perrez. His big arm reaches out for Tea's skinny shoulders, and he holds him by them. "Now you listen here, you little pip-spic! You don't come up here and tell me which end is up, hear? I *know*, hear? You don't come up in the middle of a service to the Lord and tell me which end is up, hear? I *know!* And if I want to, I can break your arms and your legs next, so you just tone your big ass down, hear? You hear?"

Tea squirms to be free, but the preacher hangs on to him. Tea says, "I said I'd give you a cut on pushing."

"If I was about to do business with you, pip-spic, you'd give me the whole cut, hear? Because I don't like your face."

"Let go me!"

"You going to listen first. Your Ace, he out! You hear? He out!"

"Whatta you mean, Preacher?"

"Ace is out! He been replaced."

"Where'd you hear that?"

"You know better than to ask the preacher a question like that."

"I don't believe you."

"In time, you will."

"So Ace is out! You're still in——you and me can make a deal. I got plenty hops depending on me. Ace got a good take on 'em. . . . You and me, Preacher, we can make a 'deal."

Preacher Rone lets go of Tea and chuckles.

"What you got against it?"

"I don't like your face."

"Level, Preacher. Level."

"Sure," Preacher Rone says, "Sure, I intend to. I was directed to. If you wants it to snow, spic, you better see a man by the name Pontiac."

"You're crazy!"

"That's right——but that don't change the facts, tamale."

"Flat Head Pontiac?"

"Ace is out. Pontiac is in. That's all the clues. That's all the news." The preacher picks up the baskets of money lying on the table near the back of heaven, and begins emptying them down his trousers pockets. Perrez stands staring at him. He murmurs, "You're lying, Preacher. You're lying!"

"You know where Pontiac live. You go ask him."

The preacher places the empty baskets back on the table, and jingles the coins in his pockets with his large hands, rocking on his heels, grinning down at Tea.

"Level more, Preacher," Tea says.

"What for? What's in it for me?"

Tea swallows. He tries to say more, but can't.

"You're just a little spic, kid. You're not a big man."

"That'll be news to the Kings, Preacher."

"The Kings? I heard the name somewhere, but I don't recall the faces. Isn't that funny? I recall most of the records, though. I recall yours in particular. Let's see, where's that farm you spent some summers—Coxsack?"

"I ain't threatening *you*, Preacher."

"You can't. Not you, snowman. Now you better shoot along. I got things to do."

Tea's voice comes out a whine. "Just tell me before I go," he says, "tell me what's going on. Can't you level that much?"

The Preacher smiles. "One does not set fire to the roof and then go to bed," he says blandly; and he turns his back on Tea, and walks through heaven toward the gold words on the pulpit that say JESUS SAVES!

If someone were to ask the girl with chestnut-colored hair, olive skin, round, frightened eyes, and a body not quite ripe yet, how old she is—they would have to ask her in Spanish. And in Spanish she would answer, "Trece." Thirteen.

But no one among the Kings of the Earth is interested in the age of the bim. She sits on the edge of the yellow-covered couch in the clubroom, listening to the raucous sounds the Kings emit on entering.

"C'mon, pay your two skins!"

"She don't look cherry to me!"

"She's tight, don't worry! Two skins! C'mon!"

"Hey hey, we gonna make a little yeabosh!"

"Two skins, pay before entering!"

"Hey, bim! Take it off, bim!"

"Wait till everybody's here. C'mon, two skins!"

"Hey, hey, we gonna git some!"

She sits silently watching the Kings saunter in, a hanky crumpled in her hand, wrinkled and damp from mopping her brow with it. The cellar is cooler than outside, but damp. Only boys are here. She must remember to be very polite, like her sister said, and then she can stay in New York and not go back to live with people who are not her blood, neighbors in Aguadilla who treated her like a *camarera,* until Rosa could send for her. Here in New York is better. See the boys all laugh and joke. Rosa said she would get money from them. Why? It is the States. *Mucho dinero!* She will help Rosa; give her it all. Will they say to her something in Spanish? What is she to do? She sits wondering.

"Okay! Everyone pay! Gonna count. Two, four, six, eight—"

"Ahora!"

"Hey bim! Bim! Don't just sit there grinning like a ninny. Take it off!"

"She don't speak English."

"Tell her in spic then!"

The Kings of the Earth circle the couch where she sits. A clock off somewhere in the distance rings midnight. In Spanish, Flash speaks to the girl, who smiles widely as he begins, *"Buenas noches!"*

She anwers, smiling, in Spanish.

"She's glad to meet us," a King guffaws.

"Get on with it, Flash!"

"All right! All right!" Flash says. Then to the girl, he says, *"Oiga,"* and she does. She listens. It does not take long to explain.

VIII

I've got some news for you
I cruise just you
I flip more than on booze for you . . .
　　—A RED EYES DE JARRO ORIGINAL.

ON WEDNESDAY it is pouring. The gutters of upper
Madison Avenue are filled with pools of filthy water. The
gray afternoon sky cracks with jagged lightning lines
and belches thunder. Marie Lorenzi sees Pontiac's convertible parked up in front of the photography store between
101st and 102nd, and she runs through the rain to her
rendezvous with him. Her kerchief soaks up the weather
and flattens her wet hair to her head. She hugs her school-
books to her plastic raincoat, and her worn-down high
heels kick up damp slime on her slacks. Her red sweater
smells the way wet wool does, and her mascara runs.
When she reaches the shop, the door swings open before her hand touches the knob, a bell tingles, and Flat
Head Pontiac smiles widely, bowing suavely.

"It's really goofing out today, isn't it, honey?" he says.

He shuts the door, and behind him a tall young nice-
looking fellow in his early thirties says, "Here, dear, let me
take those books for you. We'll put them down where
they can dry off."

"I look like a crud!" Marie sighs, as she sees herself
in the long mirror behind the counter. "God, look at
me!"

"You're easy on my eyes, honey," Pontiac tells her,
"very easy on my eyes, for sure!"

The tall young man smiles. "Want to take off your
scarf and dry it too?"

"Naw. No, thanks. My hair's all straight."

"Just as you say."

Pontiac puts his arm around Marie's shoulder. He says,
"Marie here is one of these chicks that's always sharp,

and always afraid she's not making the scene. Chicks like Marie are real crazy that way."

Marie is surprised, flattered, a little more unsure of herself now.

She murmurs, "You sure can pour it on thick, Pontiac."

"What'd I tell you, dad? She doesn't even dig my sincerity."

Pontiac puts his hand on the young man's sleeve then and with an arm still around Marie, he says, "This is Larry, honey. He owns this fine establishment."

"I'm glad to know you. I've heard a lot of nice things about you from Pontiac," Larry says.

Marie is pleased and perplexed by the cordial and polite atmosphere that exists. "The pleasure is mine," she says, stiltedly.

"Perhaps if we all go into the other room we'll be more comfortable."

"This cat's got a studio back here," Pontiac tells Marie. "Groovy, huh?"

The studio is a small, square room with white walls, a black fiber rug, and three or four black and white checkered sling chairs. There is a black couch with a tiger skin thrown across it, at the front of the room; and in the back and along the sides, various strobe lights, cameras, and photographers' lamps.

"Gee," Marie exclaims enthusiastically, "this is nice!"

"This ain't no ordinary cat, honey," Pontiac tells her.

"I'm glad you like it, Marie."

Pontiac slumps into a chair and sticks his long legs out in front of him. Marie sits down opposite him. The words to "America" are running on her wet bandana, and as she slides out of her raincoat, her soggy sweater shows a flat, shapeless bust, where it clings to her. Pontiac pulls his holder from the pocket of his blue corduroy sports coat, sticks a cigarette down in it, lights up and leans back, blowing smoke from his nostrils.

"I'll tell you what," Larry says, still standing. "I'll slip into my rain togs and run down the street for some coffee and pastry for us. You two have your little chat while I'm gone. All right?"

"Crazy!" Pontiac agrees. . . .

When Larry has left and closed the door behind him, Pontiac begins, "I guess we had better get right down to business. Are you with it, honey?"

"Sure. Babe says she is all for it, Pontiac. Babe is fed up to here with Gober. She will cooperate in every way on Friday."

"Good!" Pontiac says. "I'm glad to hear she is cutting him, because she is too nice a chick to get hung up on that sick boy."

' "Babe says something else, too, Pontiac. She says she overheard in Dirty Mac's the other afternoon that the Kings plan to jap the Jungles Friday, right after the dance."

"This I know, honey, but I am pleased to hear that Babe would pass this on to me. There is not much I do not know that goes on with the Kings. They operate very crudely. I'm hip! On Monday, for example, they shoot out that ignorant Red Eyes de Jarro to our turf to try and smell from Silly Charlie our wind. That really bugs me, that they think we'd trust a moron with our news."

"How do you know so much, Pontiac?" Marie asks reverently.

"You can buy more with money than you can with threats. The Kings don't dig this theory. That's why they're romper kids compared with the Jungles. If the Jungles have a clubroom, they pay rent for it. They don't promise protection to some old creep above the place who'd screw them for five skins."

"What do you mean?"

"There's a ventilator up in that store above the Kings' den. You can hear down it. That old creep'll let anyone listen for five skins."

"Boy, Pontiac, I've got to hand it to you!"

Pontiac laughs, stretches, and flips the ashes off the end of his cigarette. "Honey," he says, "I don't do things in a small way. I got plans. You think I'm just interested in gigging around with small-time gangs and their sick little intrigues? I'm interested in being a *big* man. My turf's going to be the world, honey. My gang's eventually going to make Murder Incorporated look like a pansy club. First I'm going to get a rep! My name's going to snag the imaginations of all the readers of the gore sheets, and they're going to wonder how come a cat like me got to be so big, so quick. My gang, honey—the Jungles—they're going to have a rep too! We start small, and we snowball. We get so big no one's going to touch us—no cop, no D.A., no judge, no F.B.I.—no cat nowhere going to touch us. But we play it smart. We treat folks nice. We don't threaten, we buy. That's the craziest, honey—buying the world. It's got a price too; don't think it doesn't."

"Yeah, Pontiac, it all makes sense. But where you going to get the money?"

Pontiac nods, grinning, and sucks in on his holder, musing a moment. "Make it, honey. Make it. And that brings to mind something else I want to discuss. As you know, we got a auxiliary gang called the Junglettes. Our chicks all belong. You know that?"

"Who don't?"

"That's playing it smart too, you see. We treat our chicks with respect. They're organized. They know they're rated high with us. Our chicks make money same as we do, and they keep what they make. We don't free-load on our chicks. The Jungles learned back in the Year One that people have got to be treated with human kindness or they'll goof on you someday when your pants are down." Pontiac frowns. "Excuse the vulgarity."

"You're smart, Pontiac. You're awful smart!"

"I wasn't born today."

"Gee—I'd sure like to be a Junglette myself."

Pontiac beams. "Honey, you can be. You can be."

"You kidding?"

"Pontiac does not gig around, honey. The Jungles want both you and Babe to team up. Of course, we like to think you'd join in on all the activities too. We'd like to be re-assured, honey."

"Sure!"

"And you'll profit by joining in too. Financially, I mean!"

"Gee, Pontiac, it sounds swell!"

"Crazy, honey! Crazy! Now if you will listen carefully, I will explain to you just one of the Junglettes activities. But before I do, you must promise not to interrupt or make your mind up until I have had my whole say. All right?"

"All right."

"Crazy!" Pontiac stands up and strolls about the small room as he talks. "I am going to explain first that our chicks are never asked to do anything sexual that would injure their reps as chicks. No grind sessions or line-ups. That's kid stuff. No prostitution. None of that. Our chicks are never asked to push horse at night, strictly in the daytime, and only if they can see pushing. If they cannot see this, they do not have to get with it. They are human beings.

"But to return to this sexual subject, which I hope is not bugging you, but it must be mentioned. As you know, Larry, here, is a fine photographer. He is all equipped. It is common knowledge that certain types of movies and photographs sell at a big price. A stag will rent such a movie for a hundred to two-fifty a night. A deck of good snaps goes for fifty per. A chick can be cut in twenty per cent on all deals she has participated in. It is easy money and there is no risk as to rep as you may think, for our boy Larry knows how to doctor such photographic undertaking so that the face does not show. The photography is shot in this very room, by Larry, with no one present but the participants. You met Larry; you know he is a nice guy. Everything is discreet. There is good dough to be had, and it is my opinion that a chick has only to gain. Well, what do you think, Marie, honey? Could you get with it? It is one of the more important activities of the Junglettes."

Pontiac is behind Marie Lorenzi, standing in back of the chair she sits in. He leans down and places his hands gently on her shoulders. "Honey? Could you get with it?"

"Gee, Pontiac—I—don't know. I mean, I never thought of nothing like that."

"There's big money. And no one's ever going to know. You should see Larry's fine Italian hand at work on these movies."

"I could sure use the money."

"And once you're in the Junglettes, honey, you're on your way. We're taking our girls up the ladder with us. I'm hip, honey! A few years of movie work, and you'll have made a pile. And our horizons will broaden, as they say in history books, and there'll be bigger deals, important deals, deals that no one dreamed of! We'll earn and we'll buy, earn and buy, until we've bought a little place called Worldsville, and we'll get wise it's no bigger than something we can hold in the palm of our hands."

"Gosh!" Marie sighs. "Gosh! I never heard anyone sound off like you can, Pontiac."

"Then you're in?"

"Yes. Yes, I'm in. I'm sick of being nobody. I'm in, Pontiac."

"And do you think Babe will buy it too?"

"I think she's sick of it the same way I am. I think she will. Gober's been giving her kicks where they hurt, and don't hurt good. I think she's ready for something better. Not just better than Gober, but same as me—better than the stinking little nowhere we live in!"

"Good chick! Good one!" Pontiac exclaims.

A voice says, "Well, everyone in here looks happy! Did we sign another starlet?" Larry enters the room carrying containers of coffee, and buns wrapped in rain-spotted tissue. "It's still coming down out there!" he says.

"Marie is with it," Pontiac tells him.

"Good, Marie. I'm glad to hear that."

Marie Lorenzi blushes. "I'll—feel sort or self-conscious—"

"Not for long. You'll be among friends," Pontiac tells her.

"Like who?"

"Me," Larry says. "I'm worse than Hitchcock. Always have to star in my own films. And—what'd you say Marie's friend's name is?"

"Babe," Pontiac says. "A nice doll."

Larry says, "Well, that would make it pretty easy the first time, wouldn't it, Marie? We'll just shoot you, me, and Babe. My wife will work the cameras. Here, try one of these fig buns . . . Ummm, they're delicious!"

The rain cannot drown the decaying stink of the apartment house, the cooking smells, the odor of too many people in too few rooms. Past the pile of refuse that is always there in the corridor, Gober leads Anita Manzi by the hand. They go up the stairs together, and outside the Gonzalves' flat, Gober says, "Let me take your raincoat, Nita. I guess the building smells, huh? I don't know. I sort of smell it, but I'm used to it."

Anita hands him her plaid coat, and says, "Wait—let me comb my hair first. You *sure* they expect me?"

"Sure."

"And it's all right, Gober? You're sure?"

"They're glad. They think it's nice for me to bring a girl home."

The walls around them are scratched with names, drawings of hearts, heads and bodies of women, and obscenities. Plaster is hanging by threads from the ceiling; the light bulb is the dimmest watt possible. Above them on the next floor, an angry mother is chasing her child up more stairs, yelling, "I'll put you in the furnace when I catch you, and shut the door!"

"It's pretty noisy today," Gober says, as he waits while Anita fusses with her hair. "It's not usually this noisy."

"Where I live, the couple upstairs are always fighting. We can hear them. They're always shouting at each other."

"You look swell. Really!"

"I'm nervous, Gober."

"So am I."

"You are? Why?"

"Search me. I don't know. I guess because I just never brought a girl home." Gober shrugs. "Well, I guess we might as well go on in."

"Is it your mother or your father who doesn't speak English?"

"My mother. But my father doesn't speak too good. Sort of broken."

"I'm ready, I guess."

"Well, we might as well. Come on."

Gober opens the door and steps into the living room. There on the antimacassar-covered sofa sit Mr. and Mrs. Gonzalves, in rigid postures, dressed in their Mass clothes. Neither one moves as their son enters with the girl and shuts the door behind them. Beside Mrs. Gonzalves, her husband looks very little and fragile. His feet do not touch the floor. His knees are crossed and his legs just hang over the sides of the sofa, the black shoes he wears shined to a high polish, his tight, ill-fitting black suit shiny from the pressing his wife gave it this morning. He has on a striped shirt and flower-splashed tie, a vest with a gold watch chain looped across it, and in the buttonhole of his coat, a paper rose.

Mrs. Gonzalves, big and obese, has on her navy blue silk dress with the rows of long beads around the neck. Her black hair is combed back neatly into a bun, and she smells of too much "Evening In Paris" perfume, which was given her last Christmas by Rigoberto. In her lap she holds the green satin pillow with the gold-sewn Mom across it.

Gober stands looking at them and they sit looking at him for a slow moment. Then, taking Anita's hand, Gober says, "Mama, Papa, this is Anita."

Anita smiles, "H-how do you do. Ah—*como está usted?*"

"*Buenos días,*" Mrs. Gonzalves says. "*Mucho gusto.*"

"Hallo!" Mr. Gonzalves says. "Take the chair, no?"

"*Haga el favor de sentarse?*" Mrs. Gonzalves says.

"I'm afraid my one year of Spanish isn't going to help much, Gober."

"She says, sit down please."

"*Si.*" Mr. Gonzalves nods. "Take the chair."

Anita walks to the large brown stuffed chair with the claw feet, sits forward in it, and pats her hair in place lightly with her fingers. Gober puts their damp coats on a wooden chair near the door, then goes across to the hassock beside Anita, and straddles it.

"Everybody's so dressed up around here. Think we were having a party." He snickers self-consciously. His mother does not understand him, but she smiles and says, "*Si!*"

"Rain, rain!" his father says. "It no stop all day."

"We really needed it, though," Anita comments.

"Huh?" Mr. Gonzalves leans forward.

"The rain. We really needed it."

"I don't," he tells her. "No like. No work in rain. No like."

"Oh, of course. I never thought of that."

"Papa hates rain," Gober says. "I can't remember it raining much back home. I don't know. Probably it did but I can't remember it ever raining much."

"No work in rain." Mr. Gonzalves says. "Rain, rain. No good."

They sit in silence for a while, Mrs. Gonzalves smiling at Anita, looking down at her hands, folded limply in her lap, then up again at Anita, smiling, then back at her hands. Her husband pulls at the gold fringe edging the pillow between his wife and him. He crosses and re-crosses his legs.

Gober says to Anita, "You want a coke?"

"No. No, thanks, Gober."

"I get cokes, Riggie." His father rises. "You stay. Talk. I get cokes."

"Do you want one, Nita?"

"Sure, I guess so."

"Okay, Papa," Gober says, as his father disappears into the small closet kitchen. "Not warm ones, Papa. I put some on ice last night."

Gober's mother reaches next to her on the end table for a small glass bowl filled with a combination of peanuts, raisins, and Rice Krispies.

"*Desea usted—*" She bends across, offering them to Anita.

"No. I—don't think so."

"*Desea usted—*" Mrs. Gonzalves repeats, continuing to hold the glass bowl out, grinning and nodding her head.

"No, mama, no!" Gober says.

"*Muy bueno,*" she persists.

Gober snaps at her, "Mama, *demasiado!* No!"

Mrs. Gonzalves withdraws her hand with a hurt look on her countenance. She stares down at the mixture, picks some up in her hand, raises it to her mouth, and then, suddenly, changes her mind. She drops what is in her hand back into the bowl, and replaces it on the end table. As she was doing this, Anita had mumbled, "But, *gracias,* anyway," but Gober's mother chose not to hear. Her feelings are hurt.

"That's Mama's trouble," Gober tells Anita, while his mother sulks on the couch. "She's touchy. She takes everything personal. She offers you something and you don't want it, you don't want her. That's the way she thinks."

"If I'd known that, I would have taken some. I'm stupid!"

"Why should you have! You didn't want any."

"But I could have—"

"Naw. What's the point? Mama's got to grow up someday!"

Mrs. Gonzalves is humming now; very quietly sitting and humming to herself. She traces the word Mom in the pillow and does not look across at her son and the girl. When Gober's father returns, holding three cold coke bottles by the neck, handing one to Gober, one to Anita Manzi, and keeping one for himself, Mrs. Gonzalves stares at him. Her eyes are at first peeved, then offended, then bitter.

"*Qué pasa?*" she demands. With her thumb she hits his bottle of coke.

"You forgot Mama, Papa. Here, Mama, take mine." Gober gets up and walks over to give it to her."

"No," she says, and in Spanish she complains, "I want mine. Not yours. Where's mine?"

"There were only three on ice," her husband tells her.

"And you three are the three? And I can go fly away. Because you three are the three. And all I do is cook around here and clean up. I am a maid, and you three are the family. You three are the three. Ah? You three!"

Gober says, "Look, Mama, look. I didn't know Papa would be home for sure. I didn't know last night it would rain today. I put three on. One for me. One for Nita. One for you."

"Ah, so! We are the three," she complains, "and your papa don't count! Is that it!"

"You just want a fight," her husband says.

"Yah, you got a fight coming too!" she shouts back.

Anita Manzi sits gripping and ungripping her bottle of coke, trying vainly to pretend preoccupation as Gober's mother and father quarrel.

"Mama, Papa," Gober pleads in Spanish. "We have a guest."

"Entertain her," his mother says. "You asked her here. You want to marry her, you might as well know to entertain her by yourself. You don't need your mother and father for that, Riggie. Go on, then!"

"Mama, I'm not marrying her. I'm only asking you to meet her."

"She's skinny and she would not cook you things I would, but go on and entertain. Have a good time. You'll never do it any younger, Riggie. Just forget all about your papa and me."

"Your mama wants a fight with me," Mr. Gonzalves says, "so she can make up in bed."

Gober sighs, and looks helplessly at Anita. "Why do they pick today to get their tempers going?" he says. "I'm sorry, Nita."

"The rain maybe did it, Gober."

"I don't know."

"You see the empty bed you have tonight!" Mrs. Gonzalves threatens her husband.

"What's it about, Gober? Is it me?"

"It's about nothing at all. It never is. It's exercise for them."

"Good! Then I have room to move for a change!" Mr. Gonzalves taunts. "You can sleep in the hall."

Anita raises the bottle and drinks some of the coke. Gober does not touch his. The arguing continues. Anita whispers, "Should I go, Gober? I think I should go."

"We're not here two minutes."

"I feel uncomfortable, as though I shouldn't be here, Gober. I could come back another time."

Mrs. Gonzalves is yelling, "Riggie come home and bring a girl friend, all ready you got someone to cook for you and pick up after your dirtiness and you tell me I should sleep in the hall, and you live off your daughter-in-law, is that your big game? You play some big games. Yah! Yah!"

"Tonight you be begging me turn over!" his father yells. "You fight so you can love better. You love better when you make up, ah?"

"Yah, yah, you cheese! You're an old man. You are too old for me!"

Anita rises. "Really, Gober. I think I'd rather go. I'll come back again."

"I'll go with you."

"All right. I—don't have to work until six."

"I'll go with you."

Gober takes her hand as they walk across to the chair where their coats lie. He is holding her coat for her when he hears his mother say, "Riggie!"

"Mama?" he answers glumly.

"What happens here? Hah? You bring your girl friend home and you don't stay five minutes. Where you going?"

"Come back," his father says. "I got some card tricks to show your girl."

"Riggie, does she dislike us for some reason?"

"No, Mama," he says, "She likes you. She just can't stay long."

"Tell her to come back, Riggie. I'll show her my recipes. She can't make *rulino*, I bet you."

Anita smiles at the Gonzalveses, who stand before the sofa now looking as bewildered and as expectant as they did when she arrived with their son.

"*Gracias*," she says. "*Gracias*."

"*Igualmente*," Mrs. Ganzalves answers, bowing a little, and smiling benignly, "*Igualmente*."

"Okay," Mr. Gonzalves waves. "No get wet in rain!"

"Buenos dias!" Anita says.

"Buenos dias!"

"Buenos dias!"

Behind them, Gober and Anita shut the door. Without talking, they go down the stairs, through the corridor, and into the entranceway. It is still pouring out. The rain whips the streets.

Gober sighs. "I guess we better wait for a while," he says in a sour tone.

"Don't feel bad, Gober."

"Mama and Papa are funny. They fight but in a way they are making up to each other all through it."

"I like them, Gober."

"I like them too. They are so kiddish, though. Sometimes I feel like the parents of them instead of the other way around."

"Gober? I have something to ask *you* now. Can you come to meet my brother Bob?"

"Sure."

"Friday night?"

"Friday! Why that night?"

"It's Bob's night off."

"I got something planned."

"Bob and his fiancée want us to come over to Bob's."

"Not Friday, Nita."

"Gober—I—I'd sort of told him we would."

"No," Gober answers adamantly. "It'll have to be another time. Friday is out!"

"Has it something to do with your gang, Gober?"

"I said it's out!"

"Then it has!"

"Friday night is out and that's that!"

"Gober, if your gang's so important—"

"What do you want from me!" Gober shouts at her. "I said I had something on Friday. You want me to change my whole life around for you! Move out of here! Quit the gang! Just change everything for someone I haven't even laid!" The last word slipped out. Gober gets red. He looks at her and in her eyes sees the word's hurt like a slap. Tears start stinging her eyes.

"You haven't even kissed me either, Gober," she says, "or do I get laid *before* I get kissed?"

"Either way you want it," Gober answers gruffly, and then, trembling, he takes her in his arms for the first time.

Outside the doctor's office, the rain lashes the window panes. The thin young girl clutches a plastic pocketbook and sits tensely in the chair, beside the doctor's desk.

"What more do you want me to say?" the doctor asks.

"I don't know. Isn't there something—"

"An abortion? No. As far as I'm concerned, anyway."

"But you know of someone? Some other doctor?"

The doctor shakes his head. "You probably couldn't afford it if I did. No, my dear, your best bet is to tell the man with whom you were intimate. You say you love him. Tell him. Marry him."

"No, no, no. Can't. You don't understand."

"I understand one thing. You're ten weeks pregnant. I don't know why some women think they're particularly noble or heroic not to mention their pregnancy to a man. Even today, a married woman was in, three months pregnant and in shaky condition. Doesn't want her husband to know. It beats me!" The doctor stands. "I'm sorry," he says. "I can't do anything more, except perhaps to caution you. Abortions cost anywhere from four hundred to a thousand dollars, depending on the doctor—if it *is* a doctor. And you can't be sure of that. *Under* that price, you take an even greater chance. Either way you endanger your health, if not your life, and you're committing a criminal act. I'm sorry to be so stern, but don't do anything foolish."

"Before I go, could I use your phone?"

"Surely."

The thin young girl walks to the window sill where the telephone directories are stacked. She pulls out the city directory and pushes the pages past Q to R. Then she runs a finger down the long column to Roan, Danl. 322W122.

IX

So say okay, say sure, say yes,
Say by the way, I too confess.
I've got some news for you . . .
—A RED EYES DE JARRO ORIGINAL.

Aᴛ Eʟ Pᴀʟᴀᴄɪᴏ, Tea buys a ticket.

"Hay un asiento reservado para esta noche?" he asks the girl in the box office of the dumpy little movie house.

"A reserved seat, ah?" she says back to him in Spanish. "Go sit in the back. I have to see. What's your name?"

"Tell her Perrez," he answers."

"Sit in the back. If there is a reserved seat an usher will let you know."

"There better be one."

"You can't predict about that," the girl tells him.

The theater is crowded because of the rain. The picture has been shown for two weeks, a Spanish-speaking romance; almost everyone there has seen it once, twice, three times before. It is great sport. Tea walks through the shabby lobby to the inside. There is a bad smell, made up of a hundred awful odors; and noise—laughter and catcalling, shushing, and hissing, and myriad conversations. A white-haired old man shuffles up to Tea as he stands in the back. The old man wears a ragged black suit, a striped T-shirt, and a band around his arm with "Acomodador" written across it. In his hand he carries a flashlight.

"Asiento?" he asks Tea.

Tea says, *"Asiento reservado!"*

"Ah, *si?"* The old man shrugs. He points to the last seat in the last row and tells Tea, "Sit there until we know."

Beside Tea in the row, a child sleeps. Next to her a young girl necks with a sailor. His hand is moving under her blouse. She moans and giggles and moans and giggles. It makes him bolder. His fingers slide to her skirt. The fat woman beside them chomps popcorn and watches them. They are better than the movie. On the screen a man in

95

a mambo band winks at a lady in a tight-fitting evening dress. She raises her eyebrow. Someone in the audience bellows, *"Cuidado!"* Tea holds his arm up to see the time on his watch. Ten o'clock. Tomorrow is Thursday. Cold turkey day. His arm knocks the child's shoulder and she wakes, pulls at the girl's blouse next to her. "Mama?"

"Go back to sleep," the girl says. She grabs the sailor's cap from his lap and puts it on the child's head. "See, you are a sailor, sleeping on a big boat!" The child does not buy this. She wants to go home. "Shut up or I'll call a policeman," her mother warns. The sailor bites the mother's ear.

"Asiento reservado?" the old usher's voice whispers in Tea's ear.

"Sí!"

"Follow me," he says to Tea.

They go up a worn staircase, into a small room behind the balcony. There are two or three chairs there, and a closed door leading into another room.

"Wait here," the usher commands. "She will see you pronto."

"Sí, gracias," Tea tells him; and the usher closes the door behind him, leaving Tea alone in the room. He does not have to wait long. The door to the second room opens and a plump woman in her mid-thirties greets Tea.

"Hello, Perrez. Long time no see," she laughs. Her height is below medium; her legs are fat and wide. She wears a beige kimono. Her hair is badly hennaed, and the part in the middle is black.

"Hello, Hazel," Tea says, following her into the second room. A convertible bed is pulled down, unmade. There are playing cards spread on it, a couple of crumpled Kleenexes, a nail buffer, a half-eaten candy bar. Beside the bed on a glass table is a bottle of gin, and a plate filled with pickles and sandwich crusts. A phonograph whines out a scratchy blues song.

Hazel flops on the bed. Tea sits in the chair next to it.

"Business good?" he asks.

"Can't complain."

Hazel has some nice rackets. She runs El Palacio for a smart money man who knows some other uses for a movie house besides showing movies. People who ask for reserved seats can arrange for a game, play a number, score, buy a girl who's game, or some "sneak" for one who's not, read

the latest news, or report it—depending on their fancies—
and accomplish sundry other illicit tasks. Besides these,
Hazel occasionally makes the scene as "the unknown
blonde woman" found in the husband's hotel room when
the wife and the private detective walk in. For this service, Hazel charges New York's incompatibly married couples fifty dollars, which is cheap enough in a state where
divorce is dependent upon one-half of the couple being
caught in a compromising situation.

"I need to score, Hazel," Tea says. "I'm all hung up."

"It's true what they say about Latin lovers, Perrez," she
answers, reaching over to put the phonograph needle back
at the start of the record. "They're smooth. They walk
into a lady's bedroom, and they know just the right words
of passion to turn on." She stretches her feet out on the
bed, kicks off a pair of soiled white mules. Her body
bulges under the kimono.

"I'm not much of a cat on the flesh kick," he says. "I
live to boot!"

"You're a tough little man, aren't you, sonny?" She
smiles at him, pats the bed with a pudgy hand. "Come on.
Sit over here. I like tough little men. Like to see their eyes
when they get sugared-up."

Tea goes over and sits on the bed. "Something happened
to Ace," he says. "Know anything about it?"

She reaches back for the gin bottle, swigs, brushes off
some that runs down her chin, and sets it back. "Oooh,
sonny, you're such a serious little Latin. Look at your eyes."
Her own eyes slide up and down Tea's lithe body, and her
mouth makes a lopsided grin.

"How'd you ever get the name Hot Hazel, anyway?" Tea
says in mock dismay.

She reaches forward and pinches his chin. Her kimono
falls open and Tea sees her breasts heaving like melons, the
nipples awake. She watches his face and laughs.

"It's hot," she says. "Why do you wear your jacket?"

"I look good in it."

"It's hot for a leather jacket like that, King Perrez."
She runs a finger along his name on the jacket. It slips
down to his thigh. She says, "If it'd stopped raining, I
would have gone out tonight, down to the soda fountain
where all the little tough boys make the lights go on and
the bells ring in the pinballs. But it didn't stop. So Hazel
had to stay in. No little tough boys. No pretty lights."

Tea knows what she means.

He never would have come to El Palacio if it were not the only place left him. Everywhere else he has tried. Hazel is why the usher at El Palacio is as old as Moses. But even a younger man is safer than a boy. Hazel's kick is kids.

Tea tries earnestly, "I've got to score, Hazel. I've got one cap home between me and a cold turkey, and half a dozen hopheads eating their knuckles right now waiting for me."

"I think that leather jacket's what makes you so tough. Using all those tough expressions. You're just a little boy, aren't you?"

She places her hand on him.

"Hazel, I'm in *trouble!* Don't you see!"

She lets her kimono fall all the way open. The whole soft round fatness of her churns. "So am I," she croons. "Don't *you* see?"

Beppo Ventura pounds his stomach until a belch roars up out of him. Dinner is over in the de Jarro flat.

In the kitchen, the occupants sit around listening to the rain. The Ricos occupy the army cot, upon which they have spread crumpled dollar bills and silver, and they count it out. It is rent night. They owe Mrs. de Jarro $50 a week, room and board.

Jesus Ventura squats on the floor by the potbelly stove, drinking and watching his youngest niece as she clears the table and stacks the dishes in the sink. Her sister, Jo, primps before a cracked mirror hanging on the back of the door, and Mrs. de Jarro, Carlos Ventura and Eyes sit around the table. In the back room, eating her meal slowly on the mattress, is Grandmother Ventura.

"You going out, Dom?" Dolores asks Eyes as she passes by him.

"Yeah, I got to see Flash. He's lending me a clean shirt for tomorrow night." Eyes emphasizes the *clean shirt* and glares at his mother.

She says, "I don't wash shirts for dirty pigs to put on!"

"You be back early, Dom?"

"It's late now, Lorry."

"You're outa luck tonight, Dolores," Uncle Jesus laughs.

Mrs. de Jarro says, "Tonight I'm going to take a walk over to the police station. I'm just going to go by that way. See what they say about someone on probation start out at ten o'clock for a night. That's what I'm going to do   tonight."

"Go ahead," Eyes says. "Get your head soaked!"

"I shoulda drowned you the day you came outa me! No wonder your father took to his heels. Nick took one look at your ugly puss and it was too much for him!"

Eyes gets up. "I'm blowing. I ain't got the rest of my life to sit and hear you sound off because you jiggled when you was drunk one night fifteen years back!"

Jesus Ventura says, "Is that that noise I hear coming from the back bedroom nights, ah? Jigglin'?"

"What you saying, Jes?" Carlos Ventura asks.

"Nothing."

"I catch them at it, I kill them!"

Dolores Ventura's face is crimson. She turns her back on the room, and runs the water in the sink, full force.

"Kill him!" Mrs. de Jarro points a finger at her son. "He's the one with the ideas. He's the smart one, he is! When I take my walk by the police station tonight, we'll see how smart he is."

Carlos Ventura repeats, "I'll kill them! I swear to that! If I ever hear that!"

Jo Ventura, his older daughter, struts across the room to him. She is his favorite; a shapely, long-legged, black-haired girl in her late teens. She runs her hand through her father's hair. "You make a fuss when there's nothing to fuss over, Pa. You listen to Uncle Jes, you believe next the stars fall in the ocean."

Carlos laughs and pulls her down to his lap. "Ah! Ah! Ah!" he says, "You're the one like your mother. A beauty who could charm vipers. You're the honey-tongued one."

In the background, the Ricos count, ". . . quince, diez y seis, diez y siete, diez y . . ."

Later, while Eyes is in the bedroom stuffing cardboard into the soles of his worn-down everyday shoes, preparing to go out, Dolores comes in and sits on the mattress. Grandmother Ventura leans against the wall still chewing her food, swallowing it, raising the fork again, and staring ahead of her blankly. She understands no English.

"Dom?"

"Yeah, honey?"

"I wish I could go with you."

"It's raining, f'Chrissake. And   it's   ten-thirty. Since

when?" He looks at her with a puzzled expression. "Uncle
Jesus bugging you, is that it? Talking that way."

"I'm just so sick of it all. This place. This kind of life.
This talk. It's like everyone here hates everyone else, and
just stays together to see how much worse they can make
it for the others. I don't know. I'm just sick, Dom."

"You're really bugged, aren't you, baby? It's the rain."

"Remember how you felt when you found out that song
business was a racket the other day?"

"Sure. It hit me below the waist. But I don't let it
get me, Lorry."

"I feel that way about everything—everything—today."

Eyes stands up and pushes his feet into the shoes, squeezing them around, forcing the cardboard to fit. "I don't let
it get me," he says, "for the simple reason it don't do no
good. I don't let it get me, and I don't give up. Like,
tomorrow night I go to that musical, I maybe learn the
angles I need to know. You don't know."

"You're really looking forward to it, aren't you, Dom?"

"Sure. I wish you was going. Flash is lending me the
works. Suit, shirt, tie—the works!"

Eyes takes his King jacket from the soot-covered, rain-
splashed window sill. He says very seriously, "Lorry?"

"Yes?"

"You remember that part in my song went like this—"
He stands stiffly in the posture he always assumes when
he sings:

> *Your lips are the sweetest lips*
> *I've ever tasted*
> *For your lips, for your kiss,*
> *I'd even get wasted.*

"Remember, Lorry?" he says.

"Yes, Dom."

"Well—Dan tells me he thinks the words are too vague.
I mean, he says people aren't gonna know what it means
to get wasted. You know?"

"Yes, Dom. You told me about it."

"Yeah. So, I says to Dan," Eyes grins at Lorry, who
smiles back faintly, "I says, who knows what ko-ko-mo
means. You know? Ko-ko-mo I love you so. You know
how Perry Como's always coming on with that. I says,
who's going to know what that means?"

Grandmother Ventura bangs her spoon on the plate.
"Take it away!" she cries in Spanish.

"All right, Nannie, for heaven's sake. You just this
second finished."

"Dan had to admit I had a point," Eyes says.

"Come home before midnight, Dom? Hmmm?"

"Lorry, Lorry—you're the only one that really wants me
around, aren't you?" Eyes touches his fingers to her
cheek gently.

"Take it away!" Grandma Ventura squeals again.

"Whenever it rains in here," Babe Limon says, "the
whole place stinks of oilcloth!"

She and Marie Lorenzi sit in the striped canvas deck
chairs in the Limon flat, chewing on popcorn and watching television, but they are growing restless now and
bored. They began their viewing at 7:30; they have
swallowed down three bottles apiece of No-Cal, and
four bags of popcorn. The ashtrays overflow with butts,
and they have both given their finger and toe nails four
coats of red polish.

"I think I seen your old lady twice in my life," Marie
says to Babe.

"Staying home gives her ants in her pants. Mom's a
chick's gotta be on the go."

"Where's she go?"

"Works all day. Then goes downstairs to the bar, over to
my aunt's, around. My aunt and her's real close. Born one
right after the other."

"Twins?"

"Naw. Just one right after the other. That's why my
dad cut out. He was mad the way she never stayed home.
Always over to my aunt's. He says to Mom, 'So why
didn't you marry Flora, you spend so much time there!' "

"You get along with her?"

"Mom? Sure. I do what I want. Last Christmas she
gets this set for the place. She can't stand TV herself.
Can't sit still without getting up and running around
unless she's gossiping. That's why she likes my aunt. They
never run out of gossip. They can't think of any that happened recent, they gossip about things happened ten
years back. This set wasn't a used set, either."

Marie reaches for more popcorn and looks carefully at
Babe's face as she leans forward.

She says, "Babe?"

"What?"

"You're not still steamed or anything at what I brought up earlier?"

"I was *never* steamed, Marie. I just refuse to have anything to do with that. What my best girl friend does I don't care. That's the way it has to be between best girl friends, but take me, Marie—I never done anything like that before. I never even been in a line-up."

"I told you that confidentially, Baby-O. Not to have you throw it in my face."

"Well, the facts are in. I never could see lowering myself."

"Flat Head says all the Junglettes got to go along with this bit. It's not like a line-up. I mean, there's nothing public about it."

"Marie, how can you ask a thing like this? What you want to do, you got every right, and I give you no argument. But you and me don't see eye to eye on matters of this nature."

"Then I got to tell Pontiac that?"

"You can tell Pontiac I consent so far as playing up to him in front of the Kings at the dance, so they can have their rumble and get it over with. But then is when I draw the line. You can tell Pontiac I am flabbergasted with this new twist you inform me of, and I punk out all the way down the line on it!"

"He's going to be a big man, Baby-O. Already he has his foot in important doors. S'afternoon I heard him on the phone down at that Larry's store, and he is sounding off like a smart money man. When he brings me home after, and my old man looks out the window and sees me stepping out of that sweet car of his, my old man almost croaked. I got some respect around the place tonight. Before I come over here, my old man asks where I'm going? I says, 'I got a date,' see? And I know from his big mouth hanging open he thinks I got a date with that Buick. And he comes on with this—he says, 'I always did my best for you, Marie. I did what a father can do!' So my old lady tells him to put down the violin, because she knows like I do the old man thinks I might be going to hook something with loot and fix him in a better pad some day. I hadda laugh at that!"

"Whatta we watching this crumby play for Marie?"

Marie reaches down on the floor under the canvas chair for the newspaper. "I'll see if there's a movie on." She adds, "You're not steamed at me, though, are you, Baby-O?"

"No. Just make it plain to Pontiac my feelings. I think we can find out faster if there's a show, turning the dials." She gets up and crosses to the television set and switches stations.

Enid Roan sits listening to her husband talk. His raincoat is tossed across his lap, his hair still damp from the downpour. He lights a cigarette and continues: ". . . so everything is in a big mess. I can't locate the Gonzalves kid or the Perrez kid. I know the Jungles and the Kings will rumble, but I don't know when. Then to top it off this girl gets herself pregnant. I thought I'd never get home tonight."

"I thought the same, Dan. I don't know." She sighs and fiddles with the wedding band on her finger. "Sometimes I think it's all futile. All of it!"

"And you think I don't?"

"Yes, but you seem to be drawn toward jobs like this. Before this, there was that miserable counselor's job in the reformatory, before that the summer at the training camp—and now gangs!"

"You certainly sound sour tonight."

"Perhaps."

"Look, Enid. I don't expect you to be as concerned with this business as I am, but it doesn't help to have you disenchanted with it, either."

"All right, I'm enchanted again. That's pretty hard too, on an empty stomach."

"When I called, I told you to eat."

"Food doesn't taste like anything when you eat it alone."

"So what am I supposed to do, Enid? Shall I neglect that Ventura girl, who's half out of her mind with worry over being pregnant?"

"She's the girl friend of Red Eyes de Jarro, isn't she? The one you're taking to the show tomorrow?"

"Yes . . . I thought of telling him, even though she doesn't want him to know. Then I decided she was probably right. First we've got to work out something for her, perhaps enter her in a home until the baby's born. She's sixteen, a young sixteen, but he's an even younger fifteen. And then there's the family to cope with. Her father—Boy, it's a mess, Enid. I just go in circles some days."

"Ummm."

"And I know this Perrez kid, the addict. I know he's lost his source, and he's off somewhere trying to connect with someone who'll give him more heroin. And Gonzalves —I want to make him see the idiocy behind this on-coming rumble, and to make him——"

Enid Roan gets up abruptly. "I'll fix something to eat, Dan," she says, but her voice breaks, and as she turns to leave the room, she hurries, hiding her face.

"Enid." Dan Roan follows her, his expression puzzled. In the kitchen, her back to him, she cries.

"Enid, what's the matter? I'm sorry I was late, honey. I told you why. You could see what I was up against, couldn't you? You know——"

"I know. I know. Rumbles and dope addicts—and the final irony. A pregnant girl who needs your help!"

"Enid, I never saw you carry on like this. Honey, what's the matter?"

"Dan, you're always so busy putting out the fires in other peoples' homes, you can't tell if something is burn-ing in your own." She turns and faces him, tears streak-ing down her face. "Dan, look at me. Look at me good."

"Honey, what is it?"

"Don't you see anything different?"

"No . . . No—you're upset, of course——"

"And I'm also three and a half months pregnant, Dan."

"Enid!"

"I've been trying to think of some way to tell you. Some way to make you glad we're going to have a child we can't afford; some way maybe to make you love it enough to want to get into some decent, respectable work, with real people—not with Black Eyes, and Tea House, and Two-gun Charlie—but with people *worth* saving. Not these beasts, not these gangs and their silly rumbles! Dan, we're going to have a child—and I'm fed up to my teeth with the Kings of the Earth!"

At midnight it is dark now and damp. The rain has stopped. The streets are black and blue. Tea walks down Park to 99th, clutching tightly to the box he got at El Palacio. His eyes water and he keeps yawning, but he tells himself he can boot up now. He got what he set out for. The memory of how he got it swims like slime in his mind; and the song that was playing on the phonograph plays its tune wordlessly, endlessly, beats its rhythm as he goes home. In between booting, life is just songs whining out the blues. In between booting no matter where you are there is a song in the background that you owe your life to.

Tea whistles it, trying not to yawn, his eyes all gooped up, dreaming of the great white mistress—snow arms that would be holding him soon, caressing him, giving him the gig. Down the crooked staircase he goes to the room in the basement; and he sees inside with the lights on, Salvadore Hostos sprawled on the bed, out, unconscious from some cheap corn that smells up the place. Tea goes past him to the dresser where he keeps the spoon, the needle, the eyedropper, and love in a capsule. He takes them and gets the water, hurrying. Then there is the sweet tension of the ritual; the match, the fluid like milk, and the jab in the thigh.

"C'mon boot!" he grins, "Boot up. Bucket! Bucket!"

And maybe a hundred years after that moment, Tea opens the little box he got at El Palacio, and he finds it stuffed to the top with lifesavers, and this note:

Perrez—Along about now you need a lifesaver. Am I rite? We figgured you'd get to Hot Hazel's in time, dad. That's the last stop, isn't it, dad. No more places. Unless you want to come into Jungle turf for a confab. And you can score in the deal. Yours truly, Pontiac.

Tea crumples the paper up in his hand, and leans back on the bed snickering to himself. Christ, it makes him laugh. The whole thing. Now he is fresh out and it's the big drought, but when he's booting, everything makes him laugh. He's even God a little.

Tea closes his eyes, giggling.

X

I'd take a lickin', dear
I'd chicken, dear
I'd punk out without any fear
If you would only say "I do"
I'd do anything you wanted me to . . .
—A RED EYES DE JARRO ORIGINAL.

THURSDAY NIGHT.

At a quarter to nine the lights dim in the St. James Theater, and the gay rhythm of the overture begins to build. Dan Roan sits in the balcony seat, not listening, his eyes fixed dully on the stage, without seeing the set as the curtain rises on it. There is a single word on his lips, a word less familiar to Roan than to Eyes, beside him—*chicken*. And this is what Roan wants to do—to chicken, to punk out, to leave the Kings of The Earth and the turmoil of their turf to some stronger zealot to resolve; to some bigger fanatic to try to handle and still have hope. . . .

Of course, Enid was ashamed after she had slept on her words. It was selfish, she had said, wrong, petty, not what she meant at all; but along with this guilt she carried, was the bulge beginning in her stomach that was something human they had created together. And now she sits at home with their child inside of her, repressing loneliness, resentment, anxiety, and the memory of a perfectly reasonable cry of protest she had made the night before. And because Dan Roan cannot let a King down—because under the law a delinquent on probation must be accompanied by a responsible adult after ten at night—Red Eyes de Jarro sits beside him, a tough kid who feels undressed without a switch-blade knife, a gang boy who would rather kill a rival in cold blood than *chicken* on a rumble, and a fifteen-year-old who unwittingly fathered a bastard.

This is a job a man can be proud of? A job that pays

104

little in cash, and less in consolation? A job that keeps him going down the depressed streets of his boyhood, searching for those boys—any one of whom might live out his adult life in Leavenworth—just as the father of Dan Roan did—trying to reason with them and find reasons for them? A job that forces him to neglect the one person in his life he loves?

"Geez, Dan, this is swell!" Red Eyes intrudes on Dan's thoughts, nudging him with his elbow, whispering.

"Yeah," Dan responds glumly. "Swell!"

Impulsively, Eyes says, "And so are you."

"Huh?" Did he hear right?

"So are you, for bringing me to it." Eyes says.

Well, that's something.

"Even though you did get the tickets for free," Eyes adds.

Around the corner from the luncheonette that night at nine o'clock, Gober stands in a doorway, watching her approach. He lights a cigarette and glances at his watch. Up in the clubroom, he knows, the Kings of the Earth will be waiting for him. He has already sent Nothin' Brown there to give the lookout, Owl, a message.

She links her arm in his when she reaches him, and they go down East 96th to Fifth Avenue.

"How much time do you have?" he asks her.

"An hour or so. Pop thinks I'm visiting a girl friend."

"I have to tell you something, Nita, something that's been bugging me. I gave it a lot of thought, and I come to a decision."

"Yes?"

"Tomorrow night I can't make it after all. I thought I could, but I can't."

"Gober, you told me yesterday you'd make it. Yesterday you told me you didn't want to have this fight, that you would tell your gang it was all off. I don't understand any of this. None of it makes any sense at all to me, Gober—these wars and all this thinking about what's the right thing to do or not. It's not right to run around fighting. Can't you see that?"

They cross the street and walk to the benches along the wall near Central Park. Gober sits beside her, a frown wrinkling his forehead, his eyes looking at the cigarette burning between his fingers. She sits sideways, facing him, an expression of sad confusion clouding her lovely face.

"Listen, Nita," Gober begins, "while I try to explain to you why I can't chicken, and I know now for sure I can't. I'd like to meet your brother—that would be swell, but—"

"Gober, it isn't just because I want you to meet Bob. I don't want you to fight. I don't want you to be written up in the newspapers like a tough fellow that runs around with gangs. I—"

"You got to hear me out, Nita, for once and for all. I run with a gang, and that's the way everybody I know runs—in gangs. I don't only run with it, and all—I lead it. I boss it! Now, you got a family and you got brothers and sisters, and I got that too; at least I got brothers, see? But mine's not like yours. Sure, I like them all right, and I'm not treated bad by 'em, and we get along. But we don't know each other so well. I mean, we don't have no business we all work at, or anything like that. You say your pop's business he worked hard for, and all of you did, and, well, in a way, it's the same with the Kings.

"See, Nita, we were just little nothings, like Nothin' Brown, for instance, who didn't belong nowhere in particular at any special time; and some of us, a whole lot of us, didn't even know the place we lived around. I mean, it was strange. You're born in this country, so it smells like your country, but when I first come here, the only thing smelled like my home was our lousy kitchen. It didn't smell or sound or look like anything but a big nowhere we was all lost in. Like a bunch of pins in a lousy haystack. Gradually we get to know a couple fellows live around us. Some that were from parts where we were, others not. But we get familiar to each other, and we sort of get glad to see each other around, because we see a lot of others traveling around together—and we hear they got clubs. The Shining Knights, the Dragons, the Blue Beards—we hear those names, and we see those guys, and we know we're different. I mean, they act like *big* guys, like they all got a secret they won't tell us, and like they don't need us to have a world. That's the impression we get. They got the world, and we're hanging on the fringes. We're on the verge of it, but we're not with it.

"So we see their jackets, and things like Blue Beard tattoos, and the Knight caps, and stuff, and we say what the hell, there's enough of us to have our own damn club. I mean, we can have an even better club if we

get organized. So we do—and that's why we give ourselves that name—the Kings—because that's the way it
strikes us. We're Kings, because we're all in on it together.
We got our own jackets, our place to meet, our ideas, our
buddies who are going to stick with us and by us, and
just, well, be Kings together."

"And fight?"

"Yes, and fight when we have to. Yes, that's part of it.
What happens to countries that don't fight for themselves?
They get taken over and stepped on. The same with
countries that don't stay tough and strong, like my home
—Puerto Rico. That's why we're nowhere today in the
world, because we weren't strong."

"America's your country, Gober! You're a citizen."

"I'm a citizen of the Kings of the Earth. That's my
country—our turf. That's where I'm home most of all,
in King turf. Not here on Fifth Avenue, or at your
luncheonette, where I have to look around all the time
to make sure your pop don't see me, or at your doctor
brother's house with his fancy—"

"Fiancée."

"I can't even say it. I don't know about things like
that. But Nita, I know the word loyalty, see? And re-
sponsibility. Those are big enough words for me . . .
Tomorrow night a Jungle's going to try to muscle in on
something that's King turf, just to see if we can hold
our turf and things that belong with it. And for me to
chicken, is for the Kings to lose their rep, a rep earned
by 'em, a rep that they gotta stand on, see? I mean, nobody's got respect for a punk, and the punk hasn't got any
for himself—and he might just as well get wasted."

"Get wasted?"

"Yeah, wasted. Just what it means: used up for no
reason—killed."

"I can't understand it, Gober, not any of it. It's all
gang stuff."

"Sure. I'm a gang guy. You got to appreciate that, Nita.
First of all, I'm a gang guy."

"And I don't matter?"

"You matter, but you don't figure. What I mean by
that is, Nita, in my life not much about you figures. Look,
you know how I feel about you. But where's it gonna
ever get me? I got to live where I live, and not forget
guys I grew with—not grew up with, or anything as

cozy, but grew with, see every day, talk the way they talk, laugh at the same things. I mean, how's it going to be any different for me? Your old man would kill me he knew we were sitting here right now. And all we're doing is talking about life and the way it works out."

"Then what's going to become of us, Gobe?"

"I don't know, Nita. Why can't we just try getting on the only way we can?"

"Because I don't want to pick up the papers and read about some boy I like and hear he's doing things against the law. Or have him tell me his gang's first."

"I go for you, Nita. I mean I even love you, or something." Gober shakes his head, drops the cigarette on the ground and squashes it. "But I got to stick by the Kings."

"What if you get picked up tomorrow, taken in by the police? What if they want to know some information about your Kings?"

"I wouldn't tell them."

"That's what I mean, Gober!" she cries. "You're blind on this subject. It's the Kings of the Earth *against* the earth. That's the way it is."

"It's the only thing I'm not blind about," Gober answers. "The Kings are my world. They're what I see when I look. Who'm I going to give away my world to? not anyone. Not the police, not anyone. Take a gang guy who won't squeal to the cops. Right away he's a juvenile delinquent a page high in headlines. But if he was a soldier, refusing to tell the enemy military secrets, he'd be a hero and they'd ride him down the avenue here. But both of them are doing the same thing—being loyal to what they know. You can't chicken on it. I'd rather die than chicken on the Kings of the Earth!"

Gober sighs and for the first time looks squarely at Anita Manzi. "Don't you see?" he pleads. "I don't want to chicken!"

At twenty minutes to ten that Thursday night, Owl pokes his head in the clubroom and states flatly, "He ain't nowhere in sight. If you ask me, he ain't comin'!"

The basement is a bedlam. Since eight-thirty the Kings have awaited Gonzalves. Butt after butt is ground into the cement floor, and a veil of smoke hangs over the heads of the boys gathered there. Among them they pass a quart of cheap gin, drinking it straight from the neck of the bottle, cursing and conversing in their staccato way, teasing the tension in themselves to mold it into a whole, into a monster that is all of them put together, and the monster is mean and angry. Their shouts rise all at once, in terse, vexed tones, complaining at the betrayal of their leader.

Then Braden stands and shouts, shaking his fists, with his face red from the blood rising up to it through his neck. "Silence! Shut up! Listen!"

The Kings quiet.

"Listen to me, all of you!" Braden stands in the center of the basement. "Gober has goofed! We're all jammed up!"

"Man, you can play that number again!"

"Eighty minutes late!"

"He's not coming. He's punking out. He's hung up on that ice cream soda bim!"

"He's screwed us!"

Braden bellows, "Will you listen? F'Chrissake, I got a suggestion. Will you listen, or will we all see each each other in hell?"

"Let him talk!" Two Heads says.

"Spill!" Blitz Gianonni agrees.

Flash tells the others, "Give him a chance to have his say."

The room is Braden's then. He can handle it. The gin is warm in his belly, sparkling words now that come out in cold, clipped sounds. He paces like Gober would, his thumbs caught in the belt loops on his trousers, his jaw thrust forward resolutely. "The consensus of opinion is," he says dramatically, "that Gober isn't showing up here for this meeting tonight. Furthermore, there is a consensus of opinion that two other very goddam important members of the Kings is also punking out of this pre-rumble confab —mainly Eyes and Tea."

Flash is cleaning his nails with a sharp-bladed hunting knife. He interrupts Braden. "I told you Eyes hadda go to the show with Roan. He sent word he's with the rumble all the way, as outlined at the last session. I'm to let him know any changes."

Braden snaps, "And Tea?"

Two Heads asks, "Where you think a hophead is when his handler cut out? Out trying to score somewhere!"

"That's my whole point in this consensus of opinion," Braden says. "We're coming apart at the seams, Kings. The sawdust is falling out. Here it is the night before a rumble, and our leader is playing potsy with some little Polack piece; one of our War Counselors is at a big bleed with a nosy social worker; and the other War Counselor is on the nod. What are we, f'Chrissake, a bunch of limp-wrist fags?"

"Looks to me like Gober's gonna chicken!" Blitz Gianonni mutters.

Two Heads whines, "Dear Emily Post, lately I am sleeping in a tent over a broad who fries eggs in a luncheonette. Please advise me what there is I can do about this situation!"

"Eyes ain't punking," Flash says. "Gober and Tea I don't know about, but Eyes is in all the way across the board!"

Braden snaps his finger at a King who holds the gin bottle. He tips it and swallows, hands it back to the King, and demands silence again. Then after more pacing, and after looking around slowly at the excited faces of the others, he says, "To sum up, men! This is the deal! We decided couple days ago a rumble is got to come off, right?"

"Right!"

"And Gober was in. He was with it like all the rest. Right?"

"Right!"

"So word spreads, see, the way word does. The Jungles know we're rumbling, though they are ignorant as to the facts that we're giving them the jap. But they expect us to rumble, and tomorrow night is when we planned, immediately after the dance. Right?"

"Right!"

"But Gober is all jazzed up in the real way over this bim. This is not like Gober, and our leadership is weak. We don't even know if it's there at all. It's a serious thing to say a man will chicken, and I don't say Gober will, but I don't say neither that Gober won't. A guy with the ga-ga juices mixing it up inside of him is no more responsible than Tea with the snow passion. And Gober is not himself. We hardly seen him all week. Right?"

"Right!"

Two Heads snarls, "What we need maybe is a new King of Kings."

"Look, Heads," Braden says, "whether that is what we need or not is not what we treat here in this meeting tonight. What we got to decide is how to get Gober back in on this rumble with his old heart beating in time, instead of all off half-cocked like he is now. We can't afford changing boats in the middle of the river. Our rep would be ruined, word got around our leader punked. We'd be worth half the price of a grind girl, word ever got out Gobe chickened. I mean, Gobe's got to show up at the dance and go through the formalities of the grudge, otherwise we got no style. What we got to do is devise a scheme to make Gober want to rumble more than rub up against that bim. Right?"

Two Heads says, "What you gonna do, cut it off him?"

"You listen to what I thought up in relation to this subject, men," Braden says, "for I think I have a scheme that will work on Gober and bring him back to the fold—but fast! And also—Blitz, will you kindly pass me the gin?—also this plan is not going to harm our morale. Things have been a little dull of late, and we might as well just work up to tomorrow's adventure in Rumblesville with a little target practice of some kind—just to more or less unify us Kings of the Earth!" Braden pauses, lifts the bottle Blitz passes forward, swallows a good three shots, and draws a deep breath before he says, "Okay, here's the strategy. . . ."

On the roof, near the drainpipe, a spotted cat has a dead rat. A wedge of light from the door behind her holds the darkness away from Dolores Ventura's outline, as she leans against the brick wall and worries. It is hard for her to believe that there is life in her womb, though the sickness of it has sent her to the employees' washroom mornings, and the anxiety over it has left her sleepless. This morning a bland priest with sinus trouble blew his nose through her confession of the sin; said for her to say her "Hail Mary," and go home and tell her mother and father immediately; said to remember the child is a Catholic; and said to sin no more but grieve at such a sin as this. And behind her in the line, others waited to unburden themselves with things they had done wrong—failure to pray, denial and doubts of God, cursing, missing Mass, thoughts, words, or actions.

This afternoon Dan Roan told her to say nothing to anyone about her condition until after the interview with the social worker set up for tomorrow. And not to feel bad, because it was a very human mistake.

"When I come home tonight," Dom had promised her this evening, "I'll know all about writing them big musicals, and you and me will be on the way to Outsville, Lorry, where we can move around a little and live it up!"

Dolores Ventura thinks of these things and stares up ahead of her at the tall buildings down Park, stretching their stories to the stars in the May night sky, at the lights in the windows of another world, and at the slice of yellow moon directly above her. She hears the sounds of buses and television sets, horns from the rivers, and whistles from the tugs there, and the noises people make living close together, hiding behind paper-thin walls from the impersonal life outside. Everything seems to shut her out; no one she can think of seems to invite her in; and Dom, who is off somewhere far away from her in his presence and his thoughts, seems to isolate her more than any other person, because he is the only thing she has to love, and now his Outsville isn't real for either of them.

So she stands there on the roof, oblivious to the fact that she is not as alone as she imagines, and to the figure behind her that blocks the light from the door as it watches her momentarily, before it starts to move toward her.

XI

I've got some news for you
I cruise just you
I even sing the blues for you . . .
—A RED EYES DE JARRO ORIGINAL.

AT MIDNIGHT, Michael Manzi turns the light switch, leaving only the neons on the signs and the clock. Coming from behind the counter, he pushes a soda cooler near the open door, out into the street. The street is not too noisy: music from the jukebox in the bar up the street, the Madison Avenue buses choking in power for the hill ahead, a man whistling *Dixie,* and some moths and night bugs whispering around the lamplight. Mr. Manzi drags the cooler near the curb, opens the valve on the bottom of it, and lets the water pour into the gutter. Then he rolls it back inside the luncheonette.

Behind him the door shuts, and strong arms grab his shoulders, forcing him backward across the cooler. A voice tells him if he screams he gets "this" in the stomach, and "this" is a knife with a six-inch sharp silver blade. Four husky teen-agers surround him.

"Give the place a work-over," one commands the others.

"What is this for?" Michael Manzi asks.

"For kicks!" is the answer, "Same as this," and the boy holding the knife in Manzi's stomach lets a fist crack across the old man's jaw.

"Come on, Jungles, let's do it fast, before the nabs smell the air!" the boy shouts at the three others. He watches them while they run through the place, ripping up the leather booths with their switch blades, cracking the mirrors with a rock-filled sock one swings around his head, tipping the juke over to pry at the lock, and running back to the kitchen and emptying big containers of food, cleansing powders, and seasonings on the floor.

113

"You like the party, dad?" the boy asks Manzi. "You like the Jungle entertainment, dad?"

"You'll pay! You'll pay for this!"

"You like another fat lip, dad?" the boy says. He punches the old man again, this time below the belly. The old man groans and writhes across the cooler's top. Blood trickles down his chin from his mouth, and on to his white shirt.

"I can't get this lock, f'Chrissake. Help me on this lock!" the boy at the jukebox calls.

"Leave the goddam thing! Empty the cash from the register—that's all the loot we need. But fix the place! Fix it pretty! And then let's cut!"

"I'll remember the Jungles," the old man murmurs.

The boys says, "Dad, I doubt it," and he gives the old man his fist in his nose, and then in his head, until he doesn't have to hold him with the knife any more, because Michael Manzi's body slumps down unconscious to the floor.

Dan Roan holds the soft and lovely naked body of his wife; his own nakedness pressed against her in the double bed. There is a closeness between them now that had begun when he arrived home from the theater that is reminiscent of previous times they had cherished, when the love of each so permeates the other in every look and word and movement that they seem one identity, a complete and beautiful being that knows no separation. They had sat together for hours in the living room, sipping wine Enid had bought on sale— "a luxury," she had laughed, "for no particular occasion—" and he had told her about his evening with de Jarro.

He had described the ill-fitting "sweet" clothes Eyes had borrowed for the event, the lilac hair lotion he had drenched himself with, and the cocky, blasé mannerisms he had attempted to affect, to shield his unsureness in those novel surroundings. He had told Enid of the dark thoughts that had invaded his mind as he sat beside Eyes, the peculiar way he had transferred their significance into the jargon of the gang—"chickening"—and discussing this with her, he had found his right perspective. The job he has to do, he believes he will do without "punking out," but no longer at the expense of this marriage he has with Enid. The child they have made will get the same

chances the children he is responsible for at the Youth
Board, so far as Roan's work with them is concerned; and
Enid will never again know the loneliness which had
forced the childish withholding of the news of her
pregnancy until it burst from her as an angry announcement, told almost in spite. Dan Roan has zeal and perhaps too much, but he is not a zealot. The changes he
would bring about among the young and tough products
of city streets must be as concrete as those streets, and
well planned and laid out. This is work for a man,
not a fanatic, and a man weighs his work and his private
life in balance.

In the darkness Enid Roan helps her husband know her,
and thinks also of the affinity they feel. And for her
own part too, there is the resolution to help him, with her
love, to do the things he can: face the insurmountable
without counting it failure, and learn, in the slow way
humans do, the difference between the two.

Their bodies sing them toward fulfillment that would
have been theirs then, if the phone had not frustrated it.

Dan's long arm fumbles for the telephone's neck.

"Dan?" the voice cracks across the wire, "Dan, is it
you?"

"Oh, no! Look, Red Eyes, I just left you!"

"Dan, you gotta come down here!"

"Where the hell have I got to come? Where the hell
have I got to come at one o'clock in the morning?"

"Mount Sinai Hospital, at the emergency ward. Jesus,
Dan—oh, Jesus!"

"What's this all about? You sound like you're—" Dan
says incredulously—"like you're—bawling."

There is a pause and then the click comes over the
phone. Dan sits staring in the darkness of the bedroom,
rubbing his eyes and passing his hands back through his
hair restlessly. *"You gotta come down here!"* The
anguished command of a King in trouble, and the shock-
ing surprise of the sound of a King's choked-back sob. . . .

Beside Dan, Enid Roan waits for him to say he has
to go someplace, but instead, he comes back to her, leaving the phone's neck off the hook on the table beside their
bed.

*Detached Dan, the fix-it man . . . The trouble with you
is you're too goddam detached . . . Chicken! Chic-ken!
Chick-en!*

There is a "crisis confab" about to start over at the Jungle Club. Flat Head Pontiac works his big, blocky body comfortably in the leather armchair's padding. The room begins to fill up with the gang members who crowd together on its studio couches, wood folding chairs, and along its bare floors. The "club" is Pontiac's brother's three-room, cold-water, walk-up flat, lodged on the top floor of a decrepit tenement on 109th Street east of Third Avenue. It is a railroad flat, with one room after the other in a row; the Jungles occupy the first room, and the ones behind them have their doors locked. In front of the door leading to the second room, Bull Rossi spreads his bulk. Pontiac talks with the Jungle's War Counselor, Blackie Buttoni, as they wait for all members to arrive and settle down.

". . . so when this Lorenzi broad gives me the clue about Baby-O Limon not digging the moving pictures, dad," Pontiac is saying, "I figure Baby-O could move me the most. As a fact, Blackie, I got eyes to make her my personal deb, here on in. A chick that don't let herself get common is the kinda chick 'at would make the scene with a cat of my caliber!"

"But Lorenzi's still gonna cooperate, isn't she?"

"Or she don't qualify as a Junglette, dad, I'm hip! I mean a bim like Marie is already used and abused goods. She's gotta do something to make the scene . . . and even at that she's not the best-stacked film queen we ever had. But Larry can fix that. She buys the routine, all right. She's got a yen for Moneysville, long as you use sugar when you describe it. She'll be a good gang girl too, as good as any of them. But Baby-O's got discrimination, dad, and that moves me."

Pontiac glances around the jammed room. A dozen Jungles sit smoking, talking in subdued voices so the landlord of the building doesn't get a complaint and have to be paid off, and waiting for things to start.

"Blackie," Pontiac says, "check with Silly Charlie and see if all the Jungles is with it."

Blackie walks to the door, stepping around the boys scattered about there, and pokes his head outside. In a second he signals Pontiac that the house is full and ready. Then Pontiac rises, and the room hushes automatically.

Pontiac assumes an oratorical stance as he surveys the expectant faces of the Jungles. They range in age from fourteen to sixteen; Pontiac is the oldest. They, like their leader, all lean toward the sweet and neat style of dress. Even on a night such as this, when they are not to a fashion show, they dress down, in subdued, conservative slacks, shirts, and socks and loafers. Their gang jackets follow suit. They are simple black sailcloth with no other emblem but a drum over the button-down breast pocket. On the drum, which is white, are their individual initials embroidered in gold. Unlike the Kings, they identify themselves no more than that, wary of the omnipresent threat of arrest, for their activities are extensive, unlike the Kings. Still in gangdom style, the initials serve to stamp them as separate beings, part of a whole. They are more orderly than are the Kings. It is Pontiac's conceit that the Jungles, under his training, have more "sav-ware fare" than any other gang in or around El Barrio.

Pontiac says, "It's not news any more that tonight the Kings of the Earth staged a crazy mutiny against dad Gober. For any who don't know, a report from our scout, Jeep, came to my hands, around twenty after ten, that a cat named Braden dreamed up a scheme he put into action shortly after, without Gonzalves knowing nothing about it. The scheme was to take four Kings and stage a bust-up in a luncheonette owned by the father of this new bim Gober is hot for. The gimmick was to pretend they were Jungles; to be sure to drop the name to the old man while they're beating him around and wrecking his "bread" so that when the nabs come and word gets around, it looks like a Jungle raid. The result is supposed to be that Gonzalves will get steamed like crazy, and jap us tomorrow like he never japped before. You want to continue this message, Blackie, while I take a breather and light up?"

Pontiac slumps back luxuriously in his leather chair and sticks a cigarette in his long, robin's-egg blue holder. Blackie saunters over to the spot beside Pontiac and carries on in less elegant stance, but with a noble effort to effect the same mannerisms as his leader.

"Well," he drawls, "Pontiac gets this news and passes it among us Jungles he can locate. So seven, eight of us show up over at the Police Athletic League and make with the basketball. This is so any ideas the nabs get we are in on the bust-up is disproved by our lively presence at P.A.L. The rest of you can probably no doubt account for where you was, too, so nobody can pin it on a Jungle.

"The reason we let the Kings go ahead is obvious. If this is the way they have to go about making the rumble a success tomorrow, then we buy it, because that rumble must come off! And it must come off formal—with the bit at the dance and all the trimmings. In addition, it will not hurt our rep any to have the newspapers writing that we Jungles are responsible for a bust-up, but no arrests are made. It doesn't hurt our rep at all. We get the credit for doing nothing. We get the glory."

"All right!" Pontiac snaps. "You made your point! Get on with the rest of the business. It is ten after one!"

"Well," Blackie continues, "mum is the word tomorrow. In fact we even act a little like we did pull the bust-up, so as to keep Gonzalves steamed. Pontiac is even going to drop a clue to Gonzalves like we might very well have done it—maybe like even Pontiac was in on it. . . . The time of the rumble is the same, right after the dance, when they plan to jap us. That too is mum! Is that the score, Pontiac?"

"Yes, from your mouth it is," Pontiac says, and he raises himself to his feet. "Now we present the surprise. Bull, bring in the first prisoner."

The Jungles remain attentive, not saying very much among themselves, as they watch Bull open the door to the second room, and from that room, yank out the shivering figure of Nothin' Brown. His eyes are wide and tear-brimmed, and his skinny knees knock together with a frightened rhythm as he stands before the Jungles.

Pontiac walks up to him and peering down at him, announces, "This cat was on his way to the Kings' place tonight when he discovers Jeep getting his ear full over the Kings' clubroom. It was necessary for us to take him hostage so the news does not leak to the Kings that we got them cased from above."

"What's he jumping around inside his pants so much," a Jungle jeers. "He gotta take a leak?"

"No, man, like—he's doing a mambo," another cackles.

"Silence!" Pontiac orders. "We don't have the whole night to burn. Besides, it is beneath our dignity, cats, to worry this jig for our petty kicks." He places a hand on Junior Brown's shoulder. "If you were a King, cat, we'd maybe have to work you over, but you're not a King. You just smell like a King from hanging around Kings."

"Man, I'm not a anything, man. I am a neutral. And my mother will be yelling to the nabs why I ain't home by now, I swear." Tears roll out of Nothin' Brown's eyes.

"And you're going home to your mother, cat, because who needs you? But before you go," Pontiac says, pulling Nothin' up by his sweater, leaning down and looking menacingly into his eyes, "there's a clue I plan to drop in your brain, for what it's worth, dad, and it's worth every crazy limb in your skinny brown frame."

"Yes sir, I knows that." Nothin' trembles.

"You know a lot, cat. You know a whole lot. So I'm gonna make a deal with you. You go out and tell what you know, and give me the pleasure of working you over. You do that?"

"No sir, I don't wanta do that, Flat Head."

"Don't get informal, colored boy!"

"No sir, Mr. Pontiac, sir. I won't again."

"So I let you go, dad, but I give you the news, didn't I?"

"Yes sir, and that's a fact."

"Because you don't button your big flabby lip, colored boy, you'll get wasted."

Nothin' whimpers, "You don't havta spell that out for me, Mr. Pontiac!"

"Okay," Pontiac says. "Vamoose!"

Nothin' darts toward the door without looking back. His hands fumble on the knob, as the Jungles watch laughing, and after he has gone, they hear his silly-scared steps clattering down the six flights like a lead-shoed dog with his tail on fire.

"You think we shoulda let him go?" Blackie wonders.

Pontiac says, "Can't take no chances with the nabs if we wanta rumble tomorrow. Besides, he's got the stuff scared outa him. And anyhow, he don't know our real secret." Pontiac chuckles, sucking in on his holder, rocking back and forth on his heels, making the Jungles wait for this one, because it's crazy to build the suspense up. Finally Pontiac says to Bull, "Okay, Bull, dad—bring in the dessert!"

The Jungles murmur as Bull Rossi walks beyond the second room into the third. Pontiac is tremendously pleased with himself as he stands waiting, whistling a little, and fingering the black string tie he wears around the collar of his clean white shirt.

From the back room they hear Bull's commands roared. "Okay, your gag's off, your hands are free. Get the rest of you free, and get up!"

"Not too rough now, Bull, dad," Pontiac calls in. "He's a sick cat, a very sick cat!"

After seconds of the sound of shuffling feet, and Bull's "C'mon, c'mon, c'mon," the Jungles see coming from the other room a slumping, medium-sized, mud-haired boy wearing a shiny black jacket with a crown on it.

"He peed in his pants," Bull says.

Pontiac says to the Jungles, "In case none of you cats ever had the privilege before, this here is Mr. D.A. Mr. Tea Bag Perrez!"

Before them Tea stands, mopping his watering eyes and running nose with his handkerchief, his hands fidgeting over his body, scratching it, his shoulders twitching.

He says, "I gotta go again, Pontiac."

"Go in your pants like you did before," Pontiac says. "Say that pretty Spanish you were saying the other afternoon to me, and go in your pants like you did before."

One of the Jungles sucks in his breath, knowing well the agony of a dope addict with the heat on him. Tea twitches again and again, and he doesn't try to control himself. He does what Pontiac tells him, muttering, "A fix, Pontiac, f'Chrissake. Can't you see that I need one bad?"

"I said to say that crazy Spanish, dad," Pontiac answers.

"Besame el culo," Tea whines sickly.

"Pontiac, you let him get away with that?" Bull Rossi laughs.

"I can't take this act," a Jungle says. "It's too hairy. Cold turkey hits me right where I live!"

"There's a purpose behind everything, cats," Pontiac tells them. "I just want to see this cat can take orders when he needs the birdie powder. Well, Perrez," Pontiac says, "repeat what you said."

Perrez cries out the Spanish.

"Kiss mine!" Pontiac roars. "C'mon, dad, I gave you a command."

Tea struggles toward him, his eyes brimming over with moisture, his nose like a dripping faucet.

"Get on your knees, dad," Pontiac tells him, "You want a courage pill, you gotta earn it!"

Tea starts to bend his knees. Suddenly, without a word

of warning, he falls back and sprawls on the floor. Body
twitching, hands ripping at his clothing, he tears under
his shirt, raking his chest with dirty fingernails until his
flesh is clawed red and beginning to bleed. Bull Rossi
moves fast, running to the second room, returning with
the tools of relief—the spoon, the eyedropper, the water,
the match, the needle, and the flake from the tall white
horse. While the Jungles watch, Bull deftly performs this
service to the dope-starved body of Perrez.

"I think we won't have any goofing from this cat,"
Pontiac says dryly.

Slowly, Perrez pulls himself to a sitting position. He begins to change back to a human being. Gradually the
wild, rolling eyes become calm, the body quiet, its twitching gone. He pulls himself to a chair a Jungle shoves at
him, and sits back.

Pontiac takes a pack of cigarettes from his pocket, and
hands one to Tea, who takes it gratefully. Tea stares
at his ripped shirt and scratched skin, and smokes the
cigarette with his head down, not looking at any of the
Jungles.

Pontiac says to Bull Rossi, "You are a very excellent skin-
popper, dad!"

Rossi grins, gratified at the approval he has won from
his leader.

"Okay, Perrez," Pontiac says, "it ought to be clear now.
You came here cause you used up all the dealers, right,
dad? By now you got the news I'm top dealer and I'm
working all over this end of town. It ought to be clear
now. In case it isn't, we're going to keep you around
overnight, and Bull here's going to baby-sit with you
tomorrow. Tomorrow night we got sort of a scheduled
performance for you, and if you cooperate, you'll get the
hop you was just now itching for and wetting your
pants over, see, Perrez?"

Tea nods. "Yes."

"That glow you got gigging around in you now last
you about seven hours, huh, dad?"

"Six or seven," Tea says.

"Well, we'll keep fixing you through the day, dad.
But you remember something," Pontiac warns. "If you
don't do your number as planned tomorrow night, you're
gonna be right where you are now. Six or seven hours
from hell, dad. Six or seven hours from hell."

In the basement of the station house, a detective works on the bleary-eyed, heavy-lidded man picked up for questioning.

"I got all night, bastard!" he growls, "so I'll just wait till you're ready to clear up this lousy story you tell!"

"What I tell is the truth," the man persists with a stale whisky breath.

The detective says, "Your story stinks! I know stories, all kinds, and you tell the kind that stinks. Start over again. When did you see her jump?"

"I was going up for air."

"I know that! You said that! You said you saw her and you said hello to her, and she sounded depressed."

"That's right. That's right. It's like I said."

The detective kicks the chair the man slumps in. "No, bastard, it's not like you said. You said you didn't say anything to her. You said it all happened too quick. You said you didn't even get near enough to call!"

The man holds his head. "I'll get you for this treatment. I'll call the newspapers!"

"I'd like to really work you over, bastard! Don't think I wouldn't!"

"I want a glass of water. I got a right to have one!"

"Sure, sure. You got a lot of rights. You got the right to stick by what you said. You said she was depressed—that she sounded depressed. Right?"

"She did."

"What's depressed mean?"

"She didn't say it. She just said hello."

"You said she didn't say anything to you."

"I'm mixed up!"

"Did she or didn't she say anything?"

"I remember now. She didn't. She was sitting there—"

"Sitting?"

"I couldn't see whether she was sitting or standing, and—"

The assistant D.A. cuts into the conversation, opens the door and and tells the detective, "Forget it!"

"Yeah?"

"She came out of the coma. They thought she was swearing. She was saying, 'No, Jesus, no!' "

"That's him?" the detective points to the man.

"Yeah. And there were bruises she didn't get falling off a roof. All along her arms. Probably backed off—scared.

Panicked and stepped back too far! Anyway, you were right. It was no suicide, but she *was* pregnant."

Ventura jerks erect in the chair. "She was what?"

"She had one in the oven," the detective snarls at him. "I suppose you don't know anything about that either! Bastard!"

Ventura clenches his fist. "That little bastard!" he shouts. "I'll get him. I'll kill him!"

The assistant D.A. says, "You've done your share of that, Ventura." To the detective he says, "She died at two-fifty. Intracranial hemorrhage. Book him on homicide."

XII

THAT DAY, Gober does not go to school. He polishes and
cleans a Smith & Wesson, up in the clubroom of the
Kings of the Earth. The gun belongs to an absentee
member of the gang, Polo Rice, who is a sophomore,
studying currently at Warwick reformatory. Even though
it is a part of the King's arsenal, it is seldom carried
during rumbles. Tonight, however, Rigoberto Gonzalves
would feel naked without it. He is that bugged.

It was while he was on his way to school that he
learned what the Jungles had done. It was a Jungle himself who tipped him off, a Jungle named Blackie Buttoni,
who swaggered up to him on the corner of 100th and
Park, and said he'd want to know, wouldn't he, that a job
was done last night on a certain soda fountain that
specialized in sweets Gober was partial to? Gober didn't
believe him. How would he know a thing like that unless
he'd done it? It was some kind of big gas Blackie was
pulling, Gober thought, and later when he collided with
Braden, Braden agreed with Gober.

124

"I didn't hear anything about it," he'd told Gober, "but if you're rifty, why'nt you check?"

Gober said why should he be rifty over it, even if it was straight dope?

Then he blew a dime on a phone call at a cigar store a block from the school. If he got an answer, he'd hang up. Couldn't be a real job if the place was working the morning after. When he got the dime back, he chucked his books under the seat in the booth, and took off up Madison.

At noon the early editions of the evening papers gave the story, but Gober had figured it out before that. He didn't need to read the Jungle credit line.

For a couple of hours he waited around the recess yard at Anita's school, and after the lunch break, he saw her and she spoke to him.

She said, "It's your fault, isn't it, Gober?"

"It wasn't the Kings," he told her.

"I know that," she said, "but it was aimed at the Kings —at the King of Kings. Am I right, Gober? Have I learned all the lessons you taught me about gangs to come up with the right solution, Gober?"

Gober just stood there. He couldn't look at her. Pretty soon she walked away, so he didn't have to. . . .

Now he sits on an orange crate in the cellar, fondling the Smith & Wesson the way he has been for hours. The late afternoon sun sneaks in through the broken window and throws a spotlight on the dust-spotted, butt-covered floor. A few Kings straggle in to leave their rumble gear, select their weapons and lay it with their gear, and hurry on out to the streets, or Dirty Mac's, or the pool hall, or home to brush up their sweet clothes for the dance to-night. Most of them have hangovers so their palaver is not any more enthusiastic than Gober's clipped responses.

"Hi, Gobe."

"Blitz."

"Everything set for tonight?"

"All set."

"You packing a piece, Gobe?"

"That's right."

"Geez! This'll be a big one!"

"That's right, Heads, a big one!"

"You talk to Babe, Gobe? She gonna be with us?"

"Doesn't matter. We'll just go through the formalities."

"Anyone seen Eyes? You seen him, Gobe?"

"No."

Braden says, "Eyes'll be on hand all right, don't worry."

"And Tea?"

"Probably still exploring snow country," Braden says. "Can't count on Tea."

"I don't worry about Tea," Gober says, "or any King! No King's chickened yet, hophead or no!"

The Kings of the Earth know that Gonzalves is his old self again.

Nothin' Brown is also on the hook from school today. Not by choice. Tied by clothesline to a chair in the Morganhotter's kitchen, he watches the huge and broad behind of his mother as she bends down to reach the bottom shelf of the refrigerator. He squirms and wiggles inside the rope, trying to make it give, so he can get free and go find Gober, and tell him what he knows. It's a mission that has got to come off, no matter what Pontiac does to him, no matter even if he wastes him, because there's one thing Nothin' Brown is that maybe nobody figured on. He is loyal. He is also bound tightly to that goddam chair.

His mother wipes the shelf out with a wet rag and turns the knob to "defrost." She says, "You is the bane my existence. I ask God only las' night what it is I ever done to deserve a chile 'at stay out two clock in the A.M. an' come home an' say he been no place when I ask him where he been. Only las' night I ask God just to tell me what I done deserve you, Junior Brown!"

"Yeah? What God say?"

"He say he wish he knew, too." Mrs. Brown empties the cube tray and continues her dissertation.

Nothin' lets her keep on talking like that, because when she talks she doesn't listen, and he eyes a paring knife on a table not far away. He could inch that chair over there, maybe, and get the thing in his mouth. He could hold it with his teeth and saw himself out of the bonds.

The whole time he has been telling Dan Roan about it, he has kept soiled hands, tracked with wet tears, covering his face, so that from the moment he began until now, Roan has not really seen the expression there. Now when he pauses, to pull the ripped and soggy Kleenex from his back pocket, he shows his face, and Dan Roan sees better than he could ever see anywhere the face of a defeated King. It is a face he has never seen before.

". . . and so," Red Eyes says, "that's what happened. That's why I called, Dan."

Roan tells him, "I'm sorry; I wanted to come. I let you down, I know, but—"

"No. No." Eyes wipes his nose. "It wouldn't have done no good anyway. I was just—I don't know—just like somebody not in his mind, see? I couldn't believe—I just didn't know who to say anything to—I kept thinking if I could say something I could make it different. But, there was her old man there, telling everybody he was gonna kill Uncle Jesus. And my old lady! What a laugh! She says they still gotta pay the rent like Lorry and her uncle was there until two others take their place. She says that when we come from the hospital. That's her news then."

"And no one knows the baby was yours?"

"No. Whatsa difference? They think like the police, that he done it—that he musta always been after her. Well, he was—but he never—"

"Eyes, I wish I could do something."

"Nobody can. Last night when I called you I thought maybe you could do something. I don't know what the hell I thought you was supposed to be able to do."

Roan offers Red Eyes a cigarette, lights it, and lights one for himself. He says, "Eyes, I want to try to explain to you why I didn't come. First, I had no idea what it was all about. My wife is pregnant. Remember I told you that at the theater. I felt that I—"

Eyes interrupts you. "You don't have to make no excuses, Dan. I thought a lot about that too. I mean, you got something that's yours, just like I had Lorry. I was always leaving her to be with the gang. I mean, she was what I had, and I was always running off." He puts his hands over his face again, and pauses, his shoulders shaking with sobs he can't control. Outside Dan's office, the phonograph blares in the background. Tears pour through his fingers and put out the flame at the tip of the cigarette he clutches. Dan smokes and waits until Eyes can continue.

Eyes says, "I was such a kid, and here's Lorry knocked up—and me talking about songs I'm gonna write. Big deal!"

He drops the wet cigarette to the floor. "No, Dan, you were right not to come. I'd never say that, I guess, but I know a lot of things now I didn't know before. I thought and thought, all last night and all today. She was what I had that was mine. The only goddam thing that was mine!"

In his lap he holds his gang jacket. He fingers it and laughs, crying at the same time. "What a King I am now without her, huh? What a big man!"

"Do the boys know, Red Eyes?"

"Them? Hell! Whatta they know! They gotta rumble to worry about!"

"And you're not going to tell them?"

"What would it mean? Some bim's uncle tried to screw her and she fell off the roof and got wasted! They didn't even know her. I never let them. She was mine, you know?"

He slaps the jacket across the chair next to him. "I can tell you one thing, though. I ain't gonna rumble. What do I wanna fight? Do I feel like fighting the whole world? Christ, I can chicken on the whole lousy world and it don't even bug me, see? Because I already punked out on the world, if you know what I mean. A guy punks out on the only thing he has, what's he care any more? It gonna bring Lorry back I go fight a Jungle? Who'm I fighting for I go fight a Jungle? The Kings? I ain't no King. Where's my goddam crown? On a lousy leather jacket! It ain't on my head, is it? It'd fall in the goddam hole I got up there!"

"Sounds like the rumble is any time now, hmm, Eyes?"

Red Eyes looks up at Dan Roan. Red's face is striped with finger marks and tear lines, his eyes a blur. A thin smile twists his lips, and his tangled brown hair falls across his forehead. "S'afternoon, when I was thinking," he says, "I thought maybe some day I'd get a job like yours. I mean, I ain't very bright or none of that, but I never had no reason listen in class. What was I supposed to hear? I thought s'afternoon, maybe your kinda job would suit me because I know things now I didn't know. I thought of that, but I thought a lot of things. So I don't know, and I don't even know I ain't gonna hang around with the Kings. I'm punking out on them and they probably won't want me around anyway. I don't know no answers right now. I ain't on anybody's

side, just like who'm I against? I don't care. If the Kings
wanta rumble, let 'em, but I ain't telling you what I know,
Dan."

"That's fair."

Eyes pulls himself to his feet. He tosses the Kleenex he
holds in his hand into Dan's wastebasket. "I ain't going
to take up all your goddam time with my sob story, Dan."

"Do you want to wash up or anything? Fix your eyes?"

Eyes shakes his head. He says, "What the hell? They
call me Red Eyes, don't they?"

XIII

Your lips are the sweetest lips
I've ever tasted
For your lips, for your kiss,
I'd even get wasted.
—A RED EYES DE JARRO ORIGINAL.

INSIDE the Aphrodite Ballroom that night at nine o'clock, there are more females than males. Half a dozen couples dance beneath the blue- and rose-colored bulbs strung from the high-ceilinged room by a wire. Their bodies undulate in time to the mambo played by a shirt-sleeved orchestra on the crepe-paper-decorated platform at the end of the hall. Around the refreshment stand opposite it, a cluster of girls, most of them with flowing skirts and tight bodices, feign interest in a hysterical conversation they pretend to be having, and eye the entrance on the one hand, and the tables along the wall on the other. At those tables sit more girls, a seemingly privileged group, for all wear white carnations in their hair and carry red leather bucket bags. Both gatherings of girls await the "fall-ins" of the Kings of the Earth, and the Jungles. Both wonder which fall-in will be the first, which the more fabulous.

Marie Lorenzi sips a Coke through a straw, standing beside Babe Limon. In addition to these two, there are in this cluster Flo Wenzel, Birdie Lyon, Ellie Sarantio, Mildred Costello, and a few more friends, classmates of Marie and Babe, girls who have been coming to the Aphrodite the same as Marie and Babe have, every Friday night. Occasionally a stag approaches and asks one from this cluster for a dance, and the pair glide on to the floor, stay for a set, and then part. It is the Kings and the Jungles who solidify things once they arrive; and it is because they are known, by sight and reputation, if not by name, by all who regularly patronize the Aphrodite, that no stag approaches Baby-O. She is known to be the

130

property of a gang leader, which stamps her inviolate to anyone but him.

Marie gives a glance toward the tables and tells Babe, "That's what I mean, Baby-O. The Jungles do things big! Them Junglettes act like queens, don't they? You don't see no one walk up to their bunch and try to horn in for a dance. They're labeled goods."

Babe wears a low-cut, off-the-shoulder sweater with rhinestones fastened all over it and no brassière under it. It is cherry-colored, and the silk skirt is full and black. Rhinestone combs hold her hair up on top of her head, and her ear lobes have dangling rhinestone earrings clipped to them. On her feet she wears her best Cuban-heeled, black patent leather shoes, and stockings, to signify the importance of the occasion. From her small, oval-shaped beaded purse, she takes a miniature bottle of cologne, and dabs some on the insides of her wrists with her fingers.

"In a matter of time, Marie," she says, "we will have no one to envy. You want some of this stuff for your wrists?"

"Thanks." Marie imitates Babe and hands the cologne back. Her get-up is not as fetching as Baby-O's, though she has added falsies to her blue satin dress and pinned a paper gardenia in her hair. There is a dark spot near the neckline of the dress where she attempted to dry-clean a stew stain with a powder she bought at the drugstore down the street.

"Word is around that Eyes de Jarro's girl friend was pushed to death off a roof last night." Marie says.

Baby-O laughs. "It wouldn't surprise me that Eyes was the one to push her. I can't wait to get a load of Gober's face when we pull the big scene on him."

"The Jungles sure got Gober coming and going, Baby-O. I mean, last night the Polack's luncheonette, and today his other chick gets taken."

"Yeah, but my pleasure is that the rumble isn't over the bust-up job, but over the fact Pontiac is making the play for me tonight. Gober is not one to let his temper cool. If the Polack had meant all that much, he would have gone for Flat Head long before this. Like this afternoon, Kings or no Kings. Gober is not one to run with the gang unless his mood is the same as theirs. Take it from me, I know."

"You would if anyone would, Baby-O!"

"Gober I know like a book. He is not the one to go around long with a chick that doesn't let him have what he wants. And Gober wants only one thing in this world from a chick! Well, he can rumble for it now that the Polack affair is cooled. May the best man win!"

Marie eyes Babe Limon with surprise. "You would go back with that louse if he did win?"

"I don't say that. I just say I am giving Gober a taste of his medicine. Hey—brace yourself!" Baby-O says, nudging Marie in the side with her elbow and watching the entrance. "The fireworks are about to commence!"

At each side of the wide inner doorway leading to the ballroom, a large plaster figure of a nude woman, reclining on a rug, greets the entrants. Before the one on the left, the social chairman of the Kings of the Earth stands surveying the room. Then he turns to the Kings behind him, and says, "All right, we're first tonight. That's as it should be. Now let's make this the best fall-in we ever had, because we all look mighty sweet. Okay, Gobe?"

"Okay, Flash."

Gober does indeed look sweet. Tonight he wears his coolest—the navy blue suit, the white-on-white shirt, the red string tie, the square-cornered handkerchief in the breast pocket, the blue suede shoes and red socks. His black hair is combed back neatly and parted evenly, and it is not lacquered.

If there is one thing in this world Gober knows how to do it is how to fall in. Stepping just inside the entrance, he takes a stand there, turned slightly to the side, facing the refreshment stand and the tables along the wall. One knee is bent, and he casually pulls back his jacket and hooks his thumbs around his bright, wide red suspenders. His face is stony, save for the gradual raising of his right eyebrow, and the gentle poke his tongue takes at his cheek inside his mouth.

A step behind him, the other Kings make a row. They match their leader's disdain with various innovations of their own; leers, grimaces, and highly individual bodily contortions.

Through closed teeth, Gober says, "Eyes ain't here, huh?"

"No," Flash murmurs behind him. "I tell you that after what happened, I don't think he'll show."

"I bet my life he does show," Gober says. "Eyes took his

wife pretty seriously, I can see that now, and it is to his credit. But Eyes would not chicken on us. He's a good King. It's Tea I worry at now."

Next to Flash, Braden speaks up. "Tea is probably cold-turkeyed right now."

"That's what I hate to imagine," Gober says.

"Well, Gobe, there's Baby-O over there, and I see she's let them out of their cages for the event. I see them bobbing around inside that sweater every time she says something to Easy Marie." Flash says. "You see her, Gobe?"

"Yeah."

"And look beyond at the chicks of the Jungles, with posies in their hair, and little Bo-peep bags. Ain't that a picture of Spring in the Rockies if you ever seen one?"

"That's a picture, all right." Gober says. He straightens and flips a cigarette from a package he pulls from his pocket. Braden is quick to scratch a match and lean forward with a light.

"Okay," Gober says in hushed tones. "We proceed as planned. After the bit by Pontiac, the formalities are over. We let on like they're not for half an hour or so, one by one gradually leaving and hiking it over to the clubhouse to change gear and get ammunition. We come on like we're sort of falling apart at the seams, like we can't handle the insult, like we're going to light out and lick our wounds in the bushes—and pull a rumble tomorrow. Don't forget to pretend we plan to get them tomorrow. Kings, we're going to jap these horny Jungles so as they can't move—but Pontiac is mine."

"You gonna use the piece on him, Gobe?"

"I didn't polish it for a display window," Gober snaps.

Behind the Kings, a huge, swarthy man wearing a white coat and black pants, says, "You guys in line for a bus or something? Move inta the ballroom and let others get by."

"Watch your tone, man," Two Heads Pigaro says back, "or you'll insult us paying customers."

"I sell some other tickets besides to youse guys," the bouncer snarls, "and I got the phone number of the police any time you don't believe me."

"Yeah, squeal and die young, fatso!"

"Remember," the man warns, "I told you once to get on inta the room and don't block passage."

"C'mon," Gober says after the bouncer is out of sight. "Let's open the curtain."

As Gober strolls leisurely across the shining waxed floor of the ballroom, the other Kings follow him pridefully. Gober lets his cigarette dangle from his lips, his arms at his sides, his fingers snapping in time with his step. He heads straight for the refreshment table, where Babe Limon stands slightly in front of the rest in that cluster. At the tables along the wall, the Junglettes watch, fascinated.

Directly in front of Baby-O, the cigarette still hanging in his mouth, Gober comes to an abrupt stop. The smoke curls up past his handsome features, and momentarily he simply looks at her through his dark, bright eyes. Baby-O looks back at him, steadily. Baby-O is no amateur at playing this game.

"I need a fresh smoke," Gober tells her.

You have to give Baby-O credit for being smooth.

Her hand reaches up to Gober's cigarette and takes it from between his lips. She brings it to her own lips, draws in on it, and then drops it to the floor. Gober crushes it with his shoe. Out of the side of her mouth, Baby-O blows smoke slowly, opening her bag and producing a fresh cigarette. This she puts in her mouth. Gober snaps a match in flame with his fingernail. She lights it and hands the cigarette to Gober.

Arrogantly Gober smiles. He flips it to the floor without smoking it. Baby-O comes on like no other chick in the world can. She steps on the red ash of the cigarette.

Then Gober says, "Ask!"

Baby-O moves closer to him. She stands with her round breasts pushing into him from under the sweater. Gober's grin broadens to an even more arrogant one than the original. He takes her by the arm, pulls her close in a dancing embrace, and whips her away from the ring of people gathered around to witness the production.

Flash sighs with awe for his leader. "You know something?" he tells Braden. "I was skeptical before we got here. You know that?"

Braden says, "Last night didn't hurt none at all. Gober needed to see the dawn again, that's all. He's behaving like a King again."

Flash says, "Naw, I mean, I was wondering if maybe Baby-O would pull something, like not come on the way she did. But she knows whose property she is."

Two Heads Pigaro says, "Yeah, lookit them out there. Wait till Pontiac gets here. What a kick! He's gonna be a two-time loser t'night!"

Blitz Gianonni rubs his hands together, glancing around at the other girls near the refreshment booth. "Refreshments, anybody?" he chortles. . . .

Gober holds Babe Limon possessively, his eyes cold, the smile gone from his mouth, his expression reverted to the same cool one he affected for the fall-in. He mamboes expertly, his body moving against hers in the necessary hot rhythm of the music. She says nothing, assuming the same disposition. The blue lights dance over the shadows of their faces. When Gober finally does concede to talk to her, he says, "Your style's up to par tonight, Babe. Keep it that way."

"Really?"

"I have a great big score to settle with the Jungles tonight, and in particular with Flat Head."

"Would I let you down, Gober?"

"You would not. But tonight I want it extra special. When you brush him, brush him!"

"Did you think I would do otherwise?"

"Chicks are funny, Baby. This afternoon I don't know how to figure it. Maybe you are pulling a fast one, I think. But when the votes are in, there is a fact about this sort of thing. And that is people stick by what they know."

"True. True."

"What do you know about Flat Head Pontiac, you'd let him cut me out? That is something about you, Baby, I learned just a second ago. You play by the rules of the game, and you play hard. Your style was never better than just then."

"That's because my heart is always in it, Gober. Like you."

Gober says, "If you can't stick by what you know, you got nothing else!"

About thirteen Jungles are gathered on a corner near the Aphrodite Ballroom, when Pontiac's sleek Buick convertible draws up to the curb.

"Here's our boy!" Blackie Buttoni shouts. "Right on the nose!"

They stand waiting as Flat Head eases himself from behind the driver's seat, and steps out of the car. Bull

Rossi slides under the wheel. Pontiac checks the back seat. Sweaters and khaki pants and sneaks are piled there, and sitting mutely beside them, Tea Bag Perrez smokes a cigarette and stares straight ahead of him.

"Okay, Bull!" Pontiac says. "You got your orders straight?"

Bull tells Pontiac, "I'll be parked at the side entrance. We'll change on the way down, them that's driving down. The others change ahead of time, coming out one by one, and head off in the same direction. Perrez is about four hours from hell now, and he don't get any birdie powder till he works for it."

"Good cat!" Pontiac says. "Take it!"

Stepping backward from the car, he raises his hand in a salute which Bull returns as he starts the motor and pulls away.

"Citizens, citizens," Jeep exclaims, "dig the outfit that is the most!"

Pontiac pretends to ignore the compliment. He sports a powder-blue linen suit, a light-blue silk shirt, a narrow white silk tie, and white buff shoes. In the lapel of his suit jacket is a white carnation. His black hair is newly brush-cut. He smells faintly of pine lotion.

"Jungles!" he says, "we got a full night and I am anxious to get started. Only one last word. The Junglette who is carrying your ammunition is the one to stay closest to. Keep your eye on her bag at all times, and by no means goof and try to take your weapon from her in plain sight of everyone. The best way is to make it look like you and her going to take a walk toward the end of the evening. Then tell her to vamoose, and you get changed."

The Jungles murmur their approval of this plan, and follow after Pontiac as he leads the way toward the Aphrodite. . . .

It is intermission when the Jungles stage their fall-in. The band has left the stand, and everyone is standing around in groups talking, pouring shots of whisky from hip-pocket bottles into Cokes and ginger ale, and waiting for just what happens then.

Gober is sitting at a table with Baby-O, Braden and Marie, when Pontiac suddenly strolls between the plaster nudes, and steps to the head of the ballroom. For the event Pontiac sports a blue cigar holder, and as he stands there he reaches in his pocket for a gold nail and a cigar and punctures the end of the cigar with the nail in a studied air of sophistication; then he lights the cigar, and rocks back and forth on his heels with his hands clasped behind his back.

"Whatta pig!" Braden exclaims.

"I been waiting for this," Gober says. He grabs a hold of Baby-O's hand and grasps it tightly, masterfully, in his lap.

Filing past Pontiac now in a single line are the Jungles. They amble blithely across the middle of the dance floor and over to the tables, where sit the smiling Junglettes. Before each one takes his place beside a Junglette, he bows exaggeratedly from the waist.

"Now ain't that just too too hoity-toity for words," Braden smirks.

"Looks like a pansy fall-in," Two Heads Pigaro says from the next table.

Then the room is tense. Pontiac is moving directly toward the table Gober and Baby-O occupy. His steps are deliberate, each one emphasized by a puff of cigar smoke.

"Give him a real brush, Baby," Gober says.

Baby-O answers, "You know me."

Then Pontiac stands with his shoulders thrown back, looking down at them.

"If the smell of my cigar is offensive," he states, "please say so."

Braden says, "It stinks, but you stink worse!"

Gober remains sullen, feigning oblivion to Pontiac's presence.

"I am directing my question to the ladies, dad."

"I *like* it, personally," Marie Lorenzi says.

Gober thinks he should have known better than to trust that box, but wait until Baby-O sounds. Gober believes it is beneath his dignity as King of Kings to notice Pontiac at all.

"I've been thinking, Marie," Pontiac says, "that maybe you would be more comfortable at another table."

"Maybe you're right," Marie says.

"Big loss!" Braden croaks.

Pontiac puts his hands on the back of Marie's chair. "May I?"

Two Heads Pigaro says, "Why not? Everybody else has."

Pontiac holds the chair back while Marie slips out of it, smoothing her blue dress with her hands, flushing excitedly, but nervously too. Baby-O seems not to be aware of any change taking place. She smokes a cigarette and stares at it wordlessly. But just wait, Gober thinks. Pontiac is taking something from his pocket. It is a piece of cellophane with a white carnation inside.

"Real flowers for a real chick!" he says elegantly.

"From a real lily!" Braden snickers.

Marie takes the flower and Pontiac points toward the Junglettes table. "Be our guest," he says.

"Thanks," Marie murmurs, walking rather awkwardly toward the seat which Blackie Buttoni leaps up to offer to her. Almost everyone in the Aphrodite Ballroom is watching the scene with intense fascination.

"And now," Flat Head Pontiac drawls, "Miss Limon, Would you care to dance?"

"Did you bring your own band too, Flat Head?" Braden says, but Gober punches him on the knee under the table. Gober wants Baby-O to turn it on Pontiac now.

Baby-O comes alive then. She turns halfway in her chair, her hand stubbing out the cigarette she is smoking. Her teeth flash in a wide, warm smile. Gober is dumfounded to hear her say, "I would."

He stays frozen to his chair while Pontiac debonairly pulls Babe's chair out, and gives her the bow-from-the-waist routine. His eyes watch dully as Pontiac takes from his lapel the carnation he wears, and hands it to Baby-O. Then, to the horrified amazement of the Kings of The Earth and the triumphant pleasure of the Jungles, Baby-O and Pontiac take to the dance floor and waltz there by themselves, without any music. . . .

It's a good thing he don't have to sit down to git where he's goin' because he couldn't if he wanted to, and that's a fact. Four times he was on the point of giving his mother the slip when the eyes she got in the back of her head seen him, and he got his behind wasted.

Now he's made the scene and he's headin' towards 102nd Street, jet-propelled.

When he sees Gober, has he got news!

XIV

This talk about juvenile delinquency running riot in asphalt jungles and blackboard jungles crops up in the news every five years or so. Each time it sounds as though the world just isn't a safe place for decent people to raise children. Well, I'm one who is a little fed up with newspaper sensationalism! A few kids go off half-cocked and make trouble—is that a jungle? Let's be realistic! There aren't any real jungles! They exist in the minds of our hungry authors and journalists!
—FROM A TELECAST OF J.P. RALEIGH'S "INSPIRATION HOUR."

ONE THING I know," Braden says as he buckles his Sam Browne belt around his waist, "is that them Jungles are gonna get the surprise of their rotten lives about one hour from now."

There are about ten Kings in the basement on 102nd Street, Gober among them. Gober is not saying much, but his eyes show the way he feels. They are like hard dark beads. He is already dressed and waiting for the others. Five or six Kings are still at the Aphrodite, keeping up a front. The ten here are to dress and plant themselves around the tenement at 109th where the Jungles always go with their bims after the dance. Then when the others change and join them, they all close in and pull the jap. Owl gets Pontiac downstairs first, by telling Flat Head Gober wants to arrange a fair fight, and Gober is waiting out front. Flat Head is one who digs the formalities and buys scenes like that. Flat Head is one who will insist Blackie Buttoni, the Jungle War Counselor, comes down with him; and waiting for Blackie is Blitz. Owl goes back up to say more should come down; and one by one the Jungles get worked over. Eventually they get the hang of things and see they are being japped, and then Rumblesville is alive.

"Remember," Pigaro warns, as he stuffs a sock with a

139

brick, "if the Junglettes take it into their heads to join
the rumble, which is not likely—but if they do, they get
the same treatment, and maybe a little fun on the side,
should time permit,"

"And also remember," Gober says, "I get Pontiac to
myself!"

"You gonna waste him, man?" Blitz asks.

"I'm going to play with him," Gober says. "If he dies
of fright, I wouldn't be surprised. But I'm not going to
fry for him, that's sure, trigger-happy though I am!"

"C'mon," Braden says. "It's ten to twelve now, and the
dance breaks in ten minutes. We gotta move!"

Their sweet clothes secure on hangers, their rumble gear
stuffed with knives, rocks, razors, can openers, and various
other crude, homemade weapons, the Kings lumber out of
the basement room and up into the warm night air. Gober
tells them, "Split up, now, so we don't look conspicuous.
And on the double. At the corner take different routes."

He keeps his hand on his Smith & Wesson, tucked in the
belt of his jeans. Leading the others, he strides down
102nd with long, resolute steps. Midway, he hears his name
being called.

"F'Chrissake!" he moans, "who the hell's yelling my
name out—"

Pigaro turns around and sees the skinny figure running
toward them in the distance, coming from Madison Avenue
as they go in the direction of Park.

Pigaro says, "Goddam that Nothin' Brown. He's got a
voice like a loudspeaker!"

"Hey, Gobe—" the voice stretches itself—"I been huntin'
you. I been huntin' you here and at the dance hall and
back here. I got see you, Gobe!"

"Oh, f'Chrissake!" Gobe moans. Then he shouts, "Shut
your mouth, Nothin', or I'll bust it open!"

But Nothin' persists. "I gotta see you!" He keeps running.

"Jesus!" Gober cusses. "Move on," he tells the Kings.
"I'll catch up. Don't forget to split by the lot at the
corner."

The Kings are almost at the corner. Gober stands impatiently waiting for Nothin' to reach him. Nothin' Brown's
legs are worn out but he makes them go, coming toward
Gober like a wild horse. When he reaches Gonzalves, he
is out of breath, ready to drop. He pants, "Listen, Gobe, I

gotta tell you somethin'—" and that is all he gets out of him before the high shouts sound from the lot at the corner of 102nd and Park. Like a whip, Gober whirls when he hears them, and starts running. He sees the shadowy forms crop up from behind the wall, pouncing on the Kings as they pass; pouncing and swinging long objects in the air over their heads, and yelling—making the rumble noises like Gober never before heard them.

Gober runs, and behind him, somehow, Junior Brown runs, falling, skinning his knees, getting up again, and running. Nothin' never stops shouting the whole way down to the lot. "Wait, Gobe! Listen! Wait—listen!"

A rock hits the street lamp and kills its light. Gober's eyes try to know the dark. He sees a King—Braden? Blitz—drop from the impact of a brick-stocking kiss. On the lot, everyone around him is falling down or knocking someone else down. He hears grunts and groans and shrill cries of pain, and he hears the yowls of victors, and he pulls his gun and keeps it under his sweater and crouches along at the side of the wall, looking for Pontiac.

"Gobe, it wasn't the Jungles!" Nothin' is yelling behind him.

He could kick Nothin' Brown's teeth in.

"Gobe, Tea done it, and—"

Goddam Nothin' Brown. He could plug him.

Then near the end of the wall, Gober hears a new voice.

"Over here, Gonzalves. Right over here. Right near the tin-can pile, Gonzalves. Get your knife out, dad!"

This is what he wanted to know.

He moves in slowly, making sure no one's behind him— no one but goddam Nothin' Brown, still squealing his guts out.

He sees a form near the pile, at the end of the wall. He goes toward it, his fingers fondling the handle of the Smith & Wesson. He figures Pontiac won't have one, but he can't figure entirely on it, because Pontiac has been known to pack a piece before. He figures he'll hold Pontiac and make him dance, before he hits him with the butt of the gun. As he gets near the form, he sees the flash of a silver blade and laughs to himself. He's got Pontiac this time.

"C'mon," Pontiac yells. "C'mon, dad!"

Gober walks slowly toward the form that is hunched

over a little, in position to spring. He keeps his hand on the trigger, and comes closer and closer.

"Gobe, Gobe, wait!" Nothin' screams. He has fallen on a rock pile there behind Gober, sprawled across it.

Gober is a few feet now from Pontiac.

"That's right," Pontiac says. "Come closer."

"Don't worry," Gober says. And he walks right up to him, with the neck of the gun pointing; and his eyes suddenly seeing the face for the first time.

"Tea!" Gober says. "Tea, what the hell! You hopped up or something? Where the Christ is Ponti—"

Pontiac says, "I'm around the wall, Gober, and to get me, you got to pass a King, Gober. A King with a knife!"

"Bags!" Gober says, letting the gun relax, "Bags! You crazy?" he says, walking toward his War Counselor.

* * * * * *

All the front pages carried the story:

TEEN KILLERS GO SOFT
AS STATE SEEKS DEATH

All trace of bravado drained away, confessed teen-age killers Alto (Flat Head Pontiac) Moravia, and his dope-ridden accomplice, Salvatore (Tea Bag) Perrez, stood ashen-faced in court Monday with remorse showing in their eyes for the gang slaying of 17-year-old Rigoberto Gonzalves and a young Negro boy identified only as Junior Brown.

Ironically, Perrez was a member of the gang known as the Kings of The Earth, and it was he who knifed to death his leader, Gonzalves, when the war broke out between the Kings and a gang known as the Jungle Boys. The "rumble" took place shortly before midnight at a vacant lot on 102nd Street and Park Avenue in Manhattan. Fourteen boys, 14 to 16 years old, were seized by police shortly after the fracas got under way. The youths were armed with knives, clubs, lead pipe, axes, and other weapons, and by the time police arrived, Gonzalves was dead from repeated stab wounds in the chest and stomach, administered by Perrez, and Brown had been shot to death by Moravia with a Smith & Wesson gun.

The quarrel was touched off by an alleged attempt on the part of Moravia to steal Gonzalves' girl friend. It was speculated that Perrez, under the influence of narcotics, was unaware of his victim's true identity. Why Moravia murdered Brown, who was a member of neither gang, was not established.

In court neither boy was represented by a member of his family. Both still wore the clothes in which they were arrested. Perrez was said to be relieved of the suffering of the dope addict with "stand-up" shots given under police jurisdiction.

As Moravia and Perrez arrived outside the courthouse, a crowd of more than 150 watched from behind barriers across the street. Moravia, at the time of their arrest the swaggering, insolent member of the twosome, in sharp contrast to the bewildered Perrez, had lost the cocksureness that had led him to exclaim on Saturday morning, "You're talking to a big man, dad!"

Quickly they were led from a detention cell to Youth Term of Magistrates Court for arraignment before Magistrate Mann on charges of homicide, and, in Moravia's case, violation of the Sullivan law as well.

Bail for each was set at $50,000.

"If you ask me who is to blame," Magistrate Mann declared, "I would say the people of the city. The press is awake, the police are, public officials are, but the public—not only the families of these two boys, but the public in general—is asleep. Until it wakes up, the situation will continue!"

The 14 other boys, members of both the Kings of The Earth and the Jungle Boys, were scheduled for hearings as juvenile delinquents, but their arraignments in Children's Court were put off until May 31.

The Brown boy, difficult to identify at the time his body was delivered to the morgue, due to the fact that he carried nothing in his clothing other than two dried-up pieces of smoked oyster, was later identified by his grief-stricken mother, Bessie Brown, domestic, who is currently under a doctor's care.

Gonzalves' mother and father, neither of whom speak English fluently, told an interpreter that they had never heard of such a gang as the Kings of the Earth. Mrs. Gonzalves, near the point of collapse, said her son had ambitions to be a professional man, and that he was engaged to marry a girl named Anita Manzi.

Emblazoned on Gonzalves black leather jacket in bright gold letters were the words: RIGOBERTO GONZALVES—KING OF KINGS.

Printed in the United States
By Bookmasters